"Fire up the searchlight," Washuta ordered. "We'll need it."

The light flared out over the snow clear back to the tree line. No way they could miss the Sea Otter now. Cadet Tyler spotted it across the frozen river.

"Take us down," Mathias clicked over his headset.

Washuta swung the chopper down about fifty yards away from the silent seaplane, Devere already at the open hatch door.

"Not much of a welcome," Tyler said, moving toward the open hatch.

The cadets split up, moving in two groups around the twin-engine Otter. Mathias reached the crew door first, popped the lever, then opened it.

"Freeze!" a command voice barked down at Mathias, the barrel of a shotgun pointed directly at him.

CODE NAME: SNOWBALL

Ned Bannister

BALLANTINE BOOKS ● NEW YORK

Cadets

RLI: $\dfrac{\text{VL: 6 \& up}}{\text{IL: 6 \& up}}$

Copyright © 1988 by the Jeffrey Weiss Group, Inc.

Produced by the Jeffrey Weiss Group, Inc.
133 Fifth Avenue
New York, New York 10003

Library of Congress Catalog Card Number: 88-91548

ISBN 0-345-35115-0

Manufactured in the United States of America

First Edition: November 1988

CODE NAME: SNOWBALL

OPERATION FILE: TALON GROUP

COMMANDER COLONEL
CHARLES LANGSTROM, U.S.M.C.

BORN:	12/1/42, Charleston, SC
DESCRIPTION:	Black, 6'2'', 198 lbs., brown eyes, black hair, shrapnel scars across chest
SERVICE:	Graduate with honors, U.S. Naval Academy at Annapolis, 1963; Commissioned U.S. Marine Corps, 1964; Three tours of combat duty, Vietnam; Purple Heart; Promotion to Special Military Intelligence, 1968; Subsequent assignments: Chile, Greece, West Germany, Panama, Philippines, Aleutian Islands
CURRENT ASSIGNMENT:	Pentagon Special Operations: TALON GROUP—ACCELERATED CADET TRAINING
EVALUATION:	Tough but fair leader; inspires respect and strong loyalty in cadet trainees; takes strategic risks; skeptical of military bureaucracy

CADET DARYL P. CRANE, U.S. ARMY

BORN: 4/3/69, DETROIT, MI

DESCRIPTION: Caucasian, 5'8'', 140 lbs., green eyes, red-brown hair

CURRENT
ASSIGNMENT: Second year, U.S. Military Academy at West Point, NY

G.P.A.:   3.43

PRIMARY SKILLS: Gymnastics, martial arts, military history

BACKGROUND: Father, ex-Army ranger, wheelchair bound due to civilian industrial accident; mother, executive secretary, General Motors, prime support; martial training began after early school gang fight

EVALUATION: Exceptional physical ability; strong leadership; lack of patience with mediocre performance; prone to fighting with peers

CADET GREGORY DEVERE, ROTC, U.S.M.C.

BORN:	8/13/69, GRAND ISLE, LA
DESCRIPTION:	Black, 6'1'', 185 lbs., black hair, hazel eyes
CURRENT ASSIGNMENT:	Second year, U.S. Naval ROTC, Marine Corps Specialization, THE CITADEL, SC
G.P.A.:	3.72
PRIMARY SKILLS:	Underwater construction and salvage; demolition; operation of marine vehicles; mechanical control systems
BACKGROUND:	Father, no military service, owns small marine service station; mother, deceased; two older sisters; offshore salvage and construction experience with local oil companies; placed fourth in national ROTC scholarship test
EVALUATION:	Excellent skills in all marine operations; superior knowledge of metalwork, salvage operations; strong leadership ability; good under pressure

CADET MARK MATHIAS, U.S. COAST GUARD

BORN: 6/17/69, MIDDLEBURY, VT

DESCRIPTION: Caucasian, 5'10'', 150 lbs., gray eyes, blond hair

CURRENT ASSIGNMENT: Second year, U.S. Coast Guard Academy, New London, CT

G.P.A.: 3.85

PRIMARY SKILLS: Computer technology; systems planning; communications technology; skiing; biathlon; competition marksman

BACKGROUND: Father, no military service, linguistics professor, Middlebury College; mother, history professor, same; no siblings; parents consented to military career after academy acceptance was secured

EVALUATION: Strong leadership potential; master strategist; prone to overanalysis of situations

CADET NICHOLAS TYLER, U.S. NAVY

BORN:	1/3/69, WASHINGTON, D.C.
DESCRIPTION:	Caucasian, 5'11'', 135 lbs., black eyes, olive complexion, black hair
CURRENT ASSIGNMENT:	Second year, U.S. Naval Academy at Annapolis, MD
G.P.A.:	3.43
PRIMARY SKILLS:	Multilingual; fluent in: French, Italian, Spanish, German, Arabic; partial knowledge of: Russian, Japanese, Portugese, and Greek; also skilled at impersonation
BACKGROUND:	Father, career U.S. diplomat; mother, society hostess; traveled with family on assignments throughout world
EVALUATION:	Strong leadership potential; extremely intelligent; undisciplined; loyal to friends; skilled at covert activities

CADET STEVEN WASHUTA, U.S. AIR FORCE

BORN:	10/21/69, TACOMA, WA
DESCRIPTION:	Caucasian, 5'9'', 150 lbs., brown eyes, light brown hair
CURRENT ASSIGNMENT:	Second year, U.S. Air Force Academy at Colorado Springs, CO
G.P.A.:	3.61
PRIMARY SKILLS:	Pilot: civilian certification in helicopter, fixed wing, prop-and-jet engine passenger plane; ultralight and glider specialist hydraulic systems; triangulation; electronic surveillance
BACKGROUND:	Father, no military experience, owner small crop-dusting company; mother, nurse; one older brother, one younger sister
EVALUATION:	Strong leadership potential; excellent flight skills; preselected for test pilot program

ONE

Night watch duty at the academy was pretty routine. It included patrolling the halls, checking all locks and windows, and making sure that the other cadets had their lights out, their music off and their butts in bed.

At 0200 hours, the third floor of Henderson dormitory was dark and quiet. The exit signs at the ends of the hallway gave off a dim red light. The only sounds were the soft hum of the electric clock near the pay phone and the dull clicks of Cadet Crane's hard rubber bootheels.

"Damn that jerk Wilson," Crane muttered under his breath as he secured the fire-exit door for the second time that night.

After all, it was Wilson who screwed up

the advance orders in yesterday's maneuvers, not him. Crane even doubled back to cover him. But when the punk tried to pin it on him with the squad leader, Crane called him out with a fast right hook. All Wilson got was half a day of R and R in the infirmary. Crane pulled a major reprimand for "conduct unbecoming a future officer of the United States Army," more demerits, and another boring tour of night duty.

Next time, he'd have to see Old Hardball. Nobody could survive that.

Crane turned the corner of the south wing and froze. At the end of the hall, the recroom light was on. He moved closer and heard the shuffling of papers. He smiled. Probably some freshman too afraid to sleep away from home. He'd surprise the kid, give him hell for breaking curfew, change his diaper, then send him off to bed.

Cadet Crane walked up to the door as quietly as he could, his heavy G.I. flashlight on high beam, ready to blind the new guy. Taking a deep breath, he stepped into the room, quickly shut the gray steel door and turned.

"All right, mister," he barked. "Party's over. Get off your—"

"My what, Cadet Crane?" General Herman Brown said, not bothering to look up from the file in his hands.

Crane snapped to attention, his flashlight hitting his head in a hasty salute. "General, sir. I thought . . . I mean . . . the light was on and . . . I mean excuse me, sir."

"Next time, recon thoroughly before taking direct action, Crane. A valuable lesson for any future officer."

"Yes, sir. Recon, sir." Crane was trying to keep his eyes focused on a small crack in the far wall.

"At ease," the general said, returning the salute.

General Herman "Hardball" Brown, the commander of the Academy, filled the large vinyl chair directly in front of Crane. Freshly shaved and in full uniform, he bit down on his trademark half-smoked cigar as he glared up at the young cadet.

"Crane, I don't much appreciate orders that get me up in the middle of the night. Never did, never will. Especially when they come from some Pentagon marine colonel about one of my cadets. You read me, mister?"

"Yes, sir." Crane still stared straight ahead. He was sweating now.

"I see from your file you had disciplinary night duty several times already this year. Eight demerits total. You have a problem with Academy rules, cadet?"

"Yes, sir . . . uh, no, sir." He knew he was in deep trouble now.

"There are several other cadets I would have chosen, had I been consulted on this one. But I wasn't, and you're it, Crane. Your orders are to change to civilian dress, assemble your personal gear and report to West Gate Six in fifteen minutes for transport."

"Permission to ask a question, sir."

"Denied," Old Hardball grunted and rose from the chair. Standing just off to Crane's right shoulder, he took the cigar out of his mouth. "Just remember one thing, mister. Classified or not, when you step off this campus, you represent this academy and the U.S. Army. Execute this operation with honor and excellence. Good luck. Dismissed."

Cadet Crane went to attention, saluted, made an about-face and walked out of the room briskly. He had only fourteen minutes to change, grab his tags and wallet, then run across campus.

West Gate Six was deserted when Crane arrived, out of breath. The guard post was empty, the light out, and the gate open. Definitely against regulations, Crane thought. Something weird was going on, and he was right in the middle of it. Special orders from the Pentagon about him? Secret operation? What did they think this was, *Rambo* or something?

His thoughts were cut short when a dark blue sedan pulled up without headlights. He walked over to the passenger side and waited. The driver was dressed in civilian clothes.

He lowered the electric window. "Crane, Daryl P.?"

"Yes, sir," he started to salute.

"Stow it and get in. We've got a chopper to catch."

Crane barely had time to close the door when the car pulled away from the curb.

After they'd left campus and passed south through Kingston, New York, it all started to sink in for Daryl. No time to tell his roommate or his family. Picked up in the middle of the night by some zombie civilian, headed who knows where. No way this had anything to do with demerits. He was into some serious stuff here.

But first, he had to find out where this guy was headed. He cleared his throat. "Excuse me, sir. But . . . where are we going?"

Without turning his eyes from the road, he pointed to a sign coming up on the right. "Camp Smith, son. That's where the chopper's waiting."

"Right, sir. But . . . uh, what's the chopper for?"

"Can't answer that. Classified. And you're on need-to-know status."

"But, what if—"

"You'll be briefed at the final drop point.

Get ready to move fast when we pass security.''

Ten minutes later, they were stopped by two MPs at the compound gate. The driver produced his orders. One MP flashed his light at Crane to verify the description on his orders: Nineteen years old, reddish-brown hair, green eyes, medium build.

"Pass through. Field four to the right, sir."

Daryl Crane's eyes were still adjusting from the bright flash when the car suddenly stopped. He could hear the whirring sound of chopper blades somewhere in the darkness.

"Move it, Crane. This bird's got a schedule to keep. And keep your head down."

The young cadet bolted out of the car, bending over as he approached the chopper. An army sergeant stood ready at the hatch door and gave Crane a boost in. The door shut immediately, and they were airborne before Crane had a chance to grab onto something. He hit the thin metal floor hard and slid into a green crate.

The sergeant leaned over to pull him to his feet. "Bench it," he yelled over the engine's roar, pointing to the flight bench suspended from the dull gray hull.

Crane moved shakily across the floor and plunked himself down. He could feel the heavy vibrations from the engines through his whole body. He looked up and saw a green canvas bag coming at him fast. His arms shot up to catch it.

"Put the chute on and strap in," the sergeant shouted. "We've got at least an hour on this baby before we drop you."

Crane stared down at the parachute in his hands, then up at the soldier adjusting his own gear. What did this guy mean by "drop"? Daryl wondered.

It was going to be a long flight.

The sun was rising in a crimson glow as the chopper touched down on a bluff overlooking the ocean. The downblast from the chopper's rotors pushed the long, green grass down into the sand as it lowered to land. A new Jeep Scout was parked off to the right, a little downslope.

When the chopper touched ground, Daryl breathed easily. At least they hadn't made him parachute out of the chopper.

Things started to happen fast. The sergeant jerked open the hatch and motioned to Crane to give him a hand with the two cargo crates near the door. The cadet shrugged off his chute, helped push them out, then jumped down.

Crane turned to salute, but the door was already shut. He crouched low and ran to the side. The chopper lifted off and was gone, leaving the cadet alone with two crates in the middle of nowhere by the sea.

Daryl sat down on the crate. He hadn't slept since yesterday night, but he wasn't tired. Too much going on. But he was hungry as hell. And it didn't look like there was a Burger King nearby.

Suddenly, he heard the roar of a car engine in back of him. He jumped up and turned to see a shiny, blue Jeep Scout tearing up the sandy slope in his direction. It leaped over the edge onto the flat top of the bluff, then raced toward him. Crane stood his ground and the Scout skidded to a stop two feet from the crates.

A tall, young guy about his own age with short blond hair and aviator shades yanked the emergency brake, jumped out of the Jeep and walked over.

"Hey, man. Your name Daryl Crane?"

Daryl paused to look him over. After what he'd been through, he wasn't giving this guy an inch.

"Who wants to know?"

"Mark Mathias, Cadet, U.S. Coast Guard," he said, pushing up his glasses and extending his hand.

"Yeah, I'm Crane," he answered, shaking the other cadet's hand. "Where the hell are we, anyway?"

"Connecticut coast, about thirty miles west of New London. Wingate Weather Station is two miles down Shore Road. That's where we're headed. Colonel ordered me to meet you and—"

"Marine colonel?"

"Yeah." Mathias looked puzzled.

"From the Pentagon?"

"Yeah. . . . Hey, what's with all the questions?"

"Nothing. Just verifying my facts. I hope this colonel's got food in the orders. I'm dying here."

"I'm with you on that. Our orders are to load these crates in the Scout and haul 'em back to the station. Briefing's at seven hundred hours. Let's hope it's after mess."

"Sounds good," Daryl said, looking down at the crates. "So, how do you want to tackle these mothers?"

TWO

"What a dump," Daryl said as he and Mathias cruised through a broken cyclone fence gate and parked in a pitted gravel lot next to a blue Chevy van.

The Wingate Weather Station looked as if it hadn't been used in years. Paint peeled off the doors and walls of the single-story concrete block buildings. The metal observation tower and dual antennae were bent and rusted. The wind sock flopped freely on unanchored wire struts. One of the windows had a crack down the middle. Not exactly what Crane expected as headquarters.

"Yeah, but that makes it perfect," Mathias answered, turning off the ignition. "It's a great cover. Nobody ever comes

11

around here. It's got its own generator." He pointed toward the smallest building across the lot. "And wait'll you see the setup inside the briefing room. Radical technology."

Crane shrugged and got out of the Scout. Mathias slid out his side and headed for the main building.

"What about the junk in the Jeep, Mathias? I thought we had to unload it in the storeroom?" Crane jogged over to him.

"Yeah, we got it here. Let's get the other guys to do their bit," Mark said and pushed open the door.

As they entered, someone yelled, "Think fast, Cadet!"

Crane ducked fast to avoid a camo helmet from hitting his head.

"Nice move, dude," some young guy in a camo flight suit said. "Pretty fast, for an East Coast boy."

"Try that again, *dude*, and you'll see some see speed," Crane came back, getting ready.

"Whooooa, I'm shaking, man. Maybe I'll have to call in for backup." The boy in the flight suit stood.

"Cut the crap, Washuta," a big black guy in fatigues and regulation T-shirt said, moving in between them. "This ain't no cowboy showdown. Man's got a right to—"

"Who asked you, Devere?" Washuta shot back.

"Gentlemen," said a tall, dark-haired kid

in a navy blue uniform jacket and stone-washed jeans, "what's needed here is a little Navy diplomacy. I suggest we pull up a box and—hey!"

A crumpled ball of paper sailed through the room and bounced off his shoulder.

The rest of the boys grabbed whatever was close and added to the show.

"So much for naval diplomacy," Mathias called out, and the rest of the room exploded with laughter, Crane included.

After they calmed down, Washuta stepped over to Daryl and put out his hand. "I like a man who can duck when it starts flying fast."

They shook hands.

"Okay, now that you guys are in love, take it out to the Scout and unload the crates." Mathias looked around the room. "Colonel'll ream us bad if we don't get this place together before briefing."

"Let's do it," the rest of the group called out.

The cadets got the supplies squared away, the computer and display materials assembled, and the field gear organized. Tyler even found the C-rations for a cold but filling breakfast of franks and beans.

At 0658, they were huddled around the PC screen playing out interactive battle strategy Mathias found on the hard disk of the PC. Crane was about to order Alpha Company against Devere's Delta Force in a pitched fight to control an important hill, and no one heard the door open.

"You're outmaneuvered, Crane. No way you can stand up against a Delta Force formation." Devere looked back over his shoulder to make his point, when he saw the silhouette in the doorway.

"ATTEN–HUT!" he yelled, jumping to his feet.

The other cadets followed, all standing stiff, their right hands in a rigid salute facing the door.

Colonel Charles Langstrom stepped into the room, shutting the door behind him. The medium-tall, powerfully built black officer walked toward the boys slowly. He inspected the organization of the different sets of gear and supplies, then spotted the computer. Moving past the boys, he put the file marked TOP SECRET he was carrying on the CRT monitor, then turned it off.

"Unauthorized use of government equipment is a court-martial offense. I want the man responsible front and center, now."

The cadets glanced at each other. No one said a word.

"Don't make me wait, gentlemen," the colonel warned.

Mathias nodded his head slightly. Each

boy took one step forward and resumed rigid attention.

Colonel Langstrom walked past Tyler and Crane and stopped in front of Mathias. His face was one inch from the cadet's nose.

"I don't tolerate insubordinates in my command, mister," he barked. "Do you understand?"

"Yes, sir." Mathias's arm was starting to hurt.

"I didn't hear you!"

"YES, SIR!" Mathias shouted sharply.

The Colonel paced back to the computer to pick up his file and glanced at his watch.

"You all are on report, pending the outcome of this operation. Right now, I've got a schedule to keep. Resume your positions and listen up."

The cadets relaxed, throwing looks of fear and relief at each other as they found seats around the room. This officer was one mean Marine.

"My name is Colonel Charles Langstrom, U.S.M.C., Special Assignment, Pentagon. All information during this briefing is classified top secret, and you are ordered not to reveal its nature to anyone, regardless of rank. Failure to comply with these orders will be considered an act of treason. Is that clear?"

"Yes, sir," the cadets said in unison.

"Each of you has been selected to take part in an accelerated cadet training program known only as the Talon Group. Your release from regular academy service is secured at a command level in response to specific operations. During this training, your unit will be expected to execute live covert missions in the service of your country. Any public exposure of your unit during those missions will be denied by the Pentagon and the United States government.

"All equipment, information and orders for the successful completion of your mission will be supplied through me. Your performance in this program will have a direct impact on your future careers in the military."

"Permission to ask a question, sir." Tyler stood.

"Granted," Langstrom answered, breaking the seal of his file.

"Will our families be informed of our special service?"

"Negative. This program is restricted and classified. In the event of field casualty, your relatives will be notified through channels once the program is secure."

Tyler ran his hand through his dark hair and sat down.

Pausing a moment for this last message to sink in, Langstrom continued the briefing.

"This mission is code-named: SNOWBALL. Eleven hours ago, a Soviet military plane on test flight in the northern Atlantic went down thirty miles from the border between Norway and northern Finland. Two Norwegian jets observed the initial descent, but lost it in cloud cover at eight thousand feet. The Norwegian pilots got a satellite fix on the down coordinates to within two miles of the crash point in the highlands. According to all reports, the Soviets do not have access to that precise information. We have the advantage of time.''

Langstrom paused. The room was silent. The cadets were tense with excitement and curiosity.

''Because of the sensitive nature of the flight information aboard this craft,'' Langstrom continued, ''the U.S. government wants the black box recovered. Visual contact with a Soviet team with a similar goal is expected.''

The boys looked at each other. This was the real thing.

''Begging your pardon, sir,'' Mathias said, resuming attention.

Langstrom nodded.

''But, there're experienced military personnel in the European sector. Would it be more effective to deploy them to the crash site?'' Mathias waited for the boom to fall.

''Correct, mister. There are skilled unit in West Germany within three hours' flight of the plane. However, to avoid a political incident, Washington wants this handled by an unknown covert team. The Talon Group fits the bill. Any other questions?''

Crane stood. ''Sir, what weapons will be issued?''

Langstrom checked his file casually, as if he knew the answer already, then looked directly at Crane. ''This is a covert recovery mission, mister. No weapons will be issued. Your orders are to avoid any confrontation with the enemy force.''

''Sir,'' Devere said, standing next to Crane, ''the briefing stated that contact with the enemy was expected. If they show up at the site—''

''You are to abort the mission and signal for pickup. This is not an academy maneuver for extra credits, mister. Or a chance to show off what you learned on the shooting range. What is at stake here is national security, pure and simple. You men got that?''

''Yes, sir!'' they shouted together. Crane and Devere sat down.

Langstrom turned to the field map display set up to the left of the computer. He spread the map out on the table and, from the file, pulled out a stack of drawings and photographs. Then he motioned for the boys to come closer.

Selecting a cutaway drawing of a jet fighter, he began. ''This is what we're after.'' His finger circled a metal box that was mounted just aft of the cockpit. ''The data recorder. The in-flight information will tell us the limitations and capabilities of the new Soviet aircraft.''

He pulled out another drawing. ''View, topside. It will still be intact, designed to survive any kind of crash. It's possible that the airframe could have collapsed into itself, like this.'' He pulled out a photo of a fighter that had crashed somewhere in the desert. ''If that happened, you'd have to get inside.''

He slid the drawings and photos into a pile and smoothed out the map. ''The crash site,'' he said, tracing his finger over the paper. ''Located on the easterly slope between these two peaks. If there's a signal beacon coming from the plane, Mathias will be able to pick it up with the equipment provided.''

Mathias nodded.

''If there isn't a signal to work off of,'' continued Langstrom, ''you'll rely on visibility and tracking.''

''What about satellite photographs, sir?'' asked Mathias.

''Negative. Since the crash, the cloud cover has been too thick. Our satellites will make two more passes before we reach the site. Our people in Denver will be able to interpret anything they pick up. We'll get the information in flight.''

Crane took a step closer to the table. ''Sir,

after we locate the plane and remove the box, how do we get back?"

Langstrom went back to the map. "Fourteen hours after your drop time, a plane will rendezvous here, thirteen miles from the site, near the fork in this frozen river. With or without you, that plane is ordered to take off. It's the only way out. The U.S.S. *Orion* will be off the Norwegian coast."

Langstrom looked around the table. "Washington doesn't want to get into a duel with the Soviets. The plan is quiet-in and quiet-out. Are there any questions?"

It was quiet. There were questions all right, too many questions, and most of them didn't have answers. So no one spoke up.

Colonel Langstrom closed the file and put it under his arm. "Cadet Mathias, front and center."

Mathias stepped out sharply and stood at attention.

"Mathias will be team commander for this mission. Following his lead, each man sound off name, academy, branch of service, and designated specialization. Be–gin!"

The boys stood on either side of Mathias.

"Cadet Mark Mathias. United States Coast Guard Academy. Artificial intelligence and communications."

"Cadet Steven Washuta. United States Air Force Academy. Pilot, certified class four, private sector, rotary, jet, and helicopter."

"Cadet Nicholas Tyler. United States Naval Academy. Political science, certified fluent in six languages with secondary knowledge of Russian."

"Cadet Gregory Devere. United States Marine Program, The Citadel, Navy ROTC. Engineering and structural integrity, marine construction and demolition."

"Cadet Daryl P. Crane. United States Army. Weaponry, military history, close quarters combat."

"Talon Group ready for final orders, sir!" Mathias barked, saluting.

"Glad to see you men remember your training. Departure time eight hundred hours. Suit up in winter camo gear, leave all ID, including tags with your clothes, and load designated supplies in the blue van out front. You will debrief with me at completion of mission. Dis—missed!"

Langstrom saluted, then walked out.

The cadets looked at each other, stunned. It all happened so fast. National security. Russians. Covert mission. No weapons. Field casualty. It was like a dream. A bad one.

"Well, you heard the colonel," Mathias said, breaking the spell.

"Aye, aye, Commander," Tyler said and gave a mock salute.

"Can it, Tyler," Devere said, moving toward him. "I don't want my butt busted or worse because you got an attitude problem.''

"Yeah. If Langstrom heard that, he'd be all over us.''

"Okay, okay. Can't you guys take a little joke,'' Tyler said, shaking his head.

"Wise up, you guys,'' Mathias said. "We've got no time for this crap. Let's just get the job done. Agreed?''

He extended his arm, open palm down. Like a huddle, the rest of the cadets complied and broke with a cheer.

THREE

Crane checked his watch. It was 0748. They had gotten their packs together and carried them outside to the parking lot. Langstrom had opened up the back of the van, and the equipment was dumped in. He tossed the keys to Mathias and walked over to his dark sedan.

"Be firm on the uphill," he said, opening the door. "The sand is soft."

"Yes, sir." Mathias hopped onto the driver's side. "Crane, up front with me. The rest of you men in the back."

The van followed Langstrom down the dune road. It took ten minutes to reach the airstrip—if you could call it that. The runway was dirt, there was no denying that, but it also included a good many ruts, weeds and a couple of bushes. A plane waited at the far end of the strip. As they drove closer, Crane looked for an insignia, some colors, or even a number. There were none of these markings.

Tyler, holding onto a crate, looked out of the small side window. "It's not the Concorde," he said.

Washuta pulled him down by the seat of his pants. "What we have waiting for us is an old Lockheed. It's powered by four turbo props. It has a range of better than five thousand miles. It can fly real slow at low altitudes and, best of all, it can take off on a strip like we have here."

Langstrom drove under the wing and stopped by the rear door. Mathias pulled up just behind and the cadets jumped out. Tyler noticed some repairs to the sheet metal in the fuselage and on the underside of the wing. He pointed this out to Washuta.

"What you have to understand here," explained Washuta, "is that these planes have seen quite a few years smuggling drugs in South America. No surprise it shows some scars. No big deal."

They headed over to the van and hoisted up their equipment.

One of the crewmen popped open the rear door and the five cadets, followed by Langstrom, climbed aboard. The plane's beat-up exterior belied the refitted, rugged interior. Dark gray metal ribs supported sturdy walls in the massive cargo area.

Just aft of the cockpit was the command station. It was hooked up with a communications board, a chart file, and some room to stand. Midsection contained a dozen fold-down bunks and a medical closet. Behind this were the jump seats. These were two lines of metal benches secured against the ribs of the plane. In between these were the equipment pallets. They were attached to the floor by quick-release bolts. In the tail section was the ramp that led to the drop door.

The gear was stowed, then all the cadets strapped themselves into a jump seat. Langstrom reached for the intercom that was mounted next to his shoulder. He pressed the button.

"All clear in the rear," he said.

Out of the speaker came the reply, "Ten four, Colonel, enjoy the ride."

One by one, the four turbo props came alive. After half a minute, the pilot brought them up to full power. The noise was intense. It came right through the metal skin of the plane. The pilot held it at that level, then released the wheel brakes, and they rolled down the choppy runway.

Crane gripped his nylon seat harness. Tyler looked down the line at Washuta and

mouthed the words "piece of junk." Devere
looked across the width of the plane. The
skin and the ribs were plainly shaking under
the load.

The plane lifted back suddenly and started
to climb. Crane counted to ten, took a deep
breath, and slowly let it out. Then he loos-
ened his grip on the harness. The noise was
really getting to him now.

Daryl looked down the line of guys tied to
the seats. To his right, on the end, was Devere. Crane got a good feeling from this guy,
though he couldn't figure out what an un-
derwater marine cadet would do in the
mountains of Finland. Next was Mathias. He
was hard to figure. He seemed to be off on
his own a lot, even when he was right there.
Then there was Tyler. Crane thought for a
moment, then it occurred to him that if
things went really wrong, if they ended up
in a Soviet prison, Tyler would be his choice
for cellmate.

On his left was Washuta. He was easygo-
ing and on target. Crane thought that when
they got back and had a few beers, he would
want Washuta to pick the place.

On the end was Langstrom. Tough as they
come, he looked about forty years old. His
accent placed him from somewhere in the
middle South. Devere could probably fine-
tune the location. But the rest of the colonel
was on "need-to-know" status. Crane knew

it was there. The man probably had a history of missions just like this one. And, as he was sitting right here, alive and healthy, they were probably all successful.

Crane leaned forward a couple of inches to get another look at the colonel. After a few seconds, he slid back.

"Nice ride, right?" Washuta yelled over the noise.

Crane flipped him a thumbs up.

The plane stopped climbing and leveled off.

Langstrom reached for the intercom again.

"How's the weather?" he asked.

"Outside the cockpit, all clear. Greenland reports clear all the way across."

Langstrom unstrapped his seat harness and stood.

"Listen up," he shouted over the drone of the motors. "The pilot reports clear weather. We will reach drop point at fourteen hundred hours. Get some sleep. Head's in the stern. Rations aft. That's all."

After Langstrom went into the cockpit, Mathias looked around at the rest of the cadets. Tyler was settling in to sleep. Crane was unbuckling his harness, probably to go to the head. Devere was adjusting his straps to his size.

These guys are good, Mathias thought. Together, they'd pull this mission off. No problem.

An alarm went off, startling the Talon Group out of their sleep. The boys quickly looked around. Three red domed lights, mounted on the ceiling of the plane, were flashing. They must be getting close.

Langstrom moved down along the row. "Thirteen hundred thirty hours," he shouted, stopping at each one. "We hit zone in thirty minutes."

He came up to Mathias. "You've got command on this one," he said. "Don't let it get away from you. Remember, the safety of your men aside, we don't want a war."

"Yes, sir," answered Mark.

Langstrom nodded and walked aft. "Listen up!" he called out.

All eyes were on Langstrom, except Tyler's. He stole a glance in Washuta's direction and yawned.

Washuta motioned for Tyler to shut up.

"Plan calls for this unit to parachute down to the site."

He paused for a moment, waiting for the mouths that had dropped open to close back up.

"Mathias will distribute the chutes."

Mark unstrapped and followed him down

to the aft section of the plane. He threw a chute at each cadet.

Langstrom picked up the last rig. "There are two straps over the shoulders, two straps across the chest, and two straps around the legs. They buckle at these points, here and here." He motioned for Mathias to demonstrate.

The cadets got out of their seat harnesses and strapped on their chutes. The rigs were heavy, weighing almost forty pounds.

Langstrom moved down the line, checking the gear and giving each connection a solid pull. When he got to the end, he said, "Primary chute is on your back. It will be attached to the jump line by a nylon cord and will open automatically when you jump. If it fails to open immediately, release the auxiliary chute on your chest. Grab this strap and pull it tree. Do not reach for this strap unless you intend to use it. If your hand is on it, the turbulence from the air will cause it to release. Two chutes will cause a bad fall. Got that?"

Mathias helped Tyler and Devere with their chutes.

"All right then," he said, moving back up the line. "You exit from the starboard side. Your equipment will come off of the center. Clip yourselves onto the jump line and then check the man in front of you. Slide your hook down to the end of the line and take a seat."

Langstrom picked up the rear intercom. "What's the E.T. to the drop?" he asked.

The reply came back. "We're about six minutes out, coming in from the west, ahead of schedule. We have just picked up the original flight path."

"Open the hatch when we get down to about two minutes."

"Will do, Colonel."

Langstrom returned the intercom to the wall. "You'll go on the first pass." He looked down the line. "Tighten up on your helmets."

He moved down the line one last time to a position on the side of the door. Then he clipped into a safety belt.

The six of them waited, watching for the red jump light to go on. The drone of the engines seemed to get louder. Each minute was like an hour.

Mathias stood the first on line. He was ready to go. He could feel it. This thing had been building for a while, and now he was pumped. It was between him, four other guys, and whatever else was outside of that door.

Another minute. Mathias cleared his throat. Devere tapped his foot, keeping time with something the rest of them couldn't hear.

Then the levers released and the jump door swung inside. Langstrom grabbed it, pulled it open, and latched it into place. The aft end of the plane was wide open now. It was cold and dark out there. The sun must have been left behind in another time zone. And the wind was whipping past them at a couple hundred miles per hour.

Langstrom raised his arms. The cadets were standing, one hand on the top rail of the seat and the other on the jump hook. Crane looked over the three pair of shoulders in front of him. He tried to see the ground, but from where he was, all that was in sight was what they had flown over ten miles back.

Langstrom waved Mathias up to the line.

"Thirty seconds," he said. Mathias signaled that he had heard. The colonel took a good grip on his waist belt. At ten, he started to count down.

". . . three . . . two . . . one . . . go!"

Mathias stepped out, with a good push from Langstrom.

"Go!"

Devere was out.

"Go!"

Crane leaped out. He hit the wind, and his feet kicked out in front. His chute popped open and pulled him up into the air. He swung on the end of the cords. Above and below him, he could see the other cadets floating through the night sky.

The mission started, and they were looking good.

FOUR

The ground was coming up fast. Mathias could clearly see the tree lines. But that's not what he wanted. The open areas, that was it. He picked one out, as if he really had a choice. It was simply the one that was down there. Crane was in line for it. So was Washuta. But Devere was drifting off to the west.

Mathias was moving in.

A few seconds later, he dropped and rolled. His feet went out and he slid down a slope. When he came to a stop, he was half-buried in snow. He got to his knees, released the buckles, and shrugged off the harness. The chute had spread out down the slope.

He reeled it in, the cords and all, and collapsed it into a ball under him.

He removed his face shield and looked around. It was quiet. Or at least it would have been quiet if he hadn't been breathing so hard. He spotted one of the guys. He bundled up his chute and cut across the slope. It was Crane.

"Did you see anyone else?" Mathias asked.

"Over there," he said, pointing to the east.

Mathias and Crane followed the direction and picked up some movement. Tyler and Washuta were seventy yards off, in an open stand of trees. Even though it was dark, the way the bare light reflected off the snow made it easy to pick out someone.

"Okay," said Mathias. "What about Devere, did he stay clear of the trees?"

"No," Crane answered. "He went in about forty yards up."

"All right. Bring in the guys over there and down the slope. We'll pick up right here just as soon as we can. I'll go for Devere."

They split up. Mathias headed into the trees, and worked his way uphill. An open chute should be easy to see, he thought, but the way the ground rose up, the treetops were not open to the sky. The white chute blended into the slopes.

Mark had walked for a couple of minutes.

He still didn't spot anything. If he just called out, he would probably get results, but the sound would carry all the way to the coast. That wasn't a good idea. No, he would stand here and use his eyes. The guy could not be far off.

A sharp crack rang through the trees. Mathias wheeled around and dropped to one knee.

He moved forward, slowly working across the slope. About thirty yards in, the ground dropped into a ravine. He got closer, working to the edge. On the other side, off to his right, he spotted Devere. He was swinging in the air, his feet about five feet off the ground. His chute had fouled in a tree. The limb snapped under the weight. Mark watched Devere use his knife to cut the main shoulder straps of his harness. He dropped to the ground.

Mathias gave a quick double whistle. Devere spotted him, returned a thumbs up, and then climbed across the ravine.

"Looks like we're five for five," Mark said, helping Greg over the edge.

"All right!" Devere said, and they slapped gloves.

They headed back through the woods, following Mark's tracks.

"That was some ride," said Devere. "I got some rush from that."

"Yeah, then you screw it up by landing in the trees." Mathias gave him a shove.

"Not so, bro'. Just part of the test—to see if I could handle it."

They broke through the tree line. Crane, Washuta and Tyler were there, waiting. The equipment packs had been divided up. Washuta was already at work. He had a map opened up on top of a pack and was plotting in points.

"I've got a good fix on our location," he said. "I've taken it off the two peaks, one to the south and that one," he pointed over his shoulder, "to the west. That puts us about here."

The spot that he indicated on the map was outside the line that defined the crash site, but not by much. "We've got a lot of ground to the north and east."

Mathias nodded. "It's good to be at one end of the zone. At least we know which way to search."

Tyler got up and dusted off his suit. "Man, it's colder than a witch's—"

"Yeah, you got that right," Devere agreed.

Mathias adjusted the bezel on his watch. By his estimate they had been on the ground for fifteen minutes. That left thirteen hours and forty-five minutes to get the job done and get out.

"Let's get it together," said Mathias.

"There's almost two inches of new snow on the trees. That means the plane could be dusted over and hard to spot. Look for broken trees or burn marks."

They stashed the chutes and got things going. Mark split them up and spread them out over two hundred yards. It would give them a better chance of seeing something and help make their tracks difficult to see from the air.

As Washuta put it, "They would tear up the snow so much, people might think a herd of buffalo were migrating through Finland."

They worked their way to the north. The ground rose steadily as they went. They were careful to stay out of the open. Forty miles to the west, some fishing towns were stuck on the coast. Thirty miles to the east was the Soviet border. So far, no one knew about them. At least no flares went up when they hit the ground. They were making good time.

Mathias was the one who saw them first.

They had been working north along the crest of a ridge, about four miles from where they had started. The sky still had that weird glow that reflected off the snow like moonlight.

Mathias lifted the binoculars and focused up along the ridge. He worked them over the ground and between the trees, looking for something that didn't belong. Anything that could be out of place.

He liked what he was doing. The mountains of Finland were a lot like the ones in Vermont. Halfway around the world, he felt right at home.

He focused the glasses further out and checked along the ledge at 1,000 yards. When he was satisfied that nothing was there, he swung them over to the east. The soft light brought out the shape of the land. If there was something out there, it would show up.

It stood out like a four-lane highway. About a hundred yards out, a clear and distinct line had been cut through the snow. It snaked down the ridge, disappearing into a hollow, then skirting behind a stand of trees. Mathias traced it as far as he could, until it slipped over a rise and disappeared from view.

He pulled out his glasses for a closer look. He couldn't tell what had made the tracks, but there they were. He turned and looked up the ridge. Devere and Washuta were the next guys up. They were only about forty yards away, but they were searching in the wrong direction.

Mathias scrambled up to their position.

"We might have some company," he said quickly. "About one hundred yards out."

"What did you see?" asked Washuta.

"No movement," answered Mathias, "but the tracks are there. They run parallel to ours. I can't tell if we're being watched, or if we just passed somebody going the other way."

Washuta shielded his eyes. "Could be reindeer or something, right?"

"Well, I don't know," answered Mathias. "We got to get a little closer. Devere, pass the word that me and Washuta are cutting down to check it out."

Washuta nodded. "Crane and Tyler know that we're cutting down the hill to check this thing out. If we're not back in ten minutes, they'll know that something has happened."

"If it does," said Devere, "we'll be there."

"Hell, don't do that," Washuta said. "Save yourself, get back home, make up a good long story about us." He tapped Mathias on the shoulder. "Come on, Mountain Man," he said. "Let's go check on these rabbit tracks."

The two of them angled down the slope toward the line of tracks. Washuta's eyes were straight ahead. Mathias looked everywhere else. If someone was still in the area, they wouldn't be sitting alongside of their own tracks. They'd circle up to the next ridge and keep watch from a safe distance.

They reached the tracks and stopped.

"Bigger than a rabbit," said Washuta, kneeling alongside, "but smaller than Bigfoot."

"About a size eight or size nine," answered Mathias, "and heading south."

"Then if we're going in different directions," said Washuta, "they can't be tailing us."

"No, probably not," said Mathias.

He got up and followed the tracks, matching his stride against theirs. They were not as tall as he was, but there was something else. The boots were wrong. Mathias stopped short. He called back to Washuta.

"How do you get prints left in the snow that don't have any tread on them?"

Washuta's round face wrinkled up. "What is this?" he asked. "Joke time?"

"Not here," Mathias answered patiently. "See for yourself."

Washuta knelt down in the snow and took a good look.

"You've got sharp eyes, Mountain Man," he said, tracing the outline of the print. "But who'd be dumb enough to wear smooth-bottom shoes out here?"

"And that's exactly my point," said Mathias. "If you're going cross-country, you take care of your feet."

"It's the Soviet pilot," Washuta said. "His plane started to tumble, he had to get out.

He popped off the canopy and ejected. He came down wearing his helmet, flight suit, and smooth-bottom flight boots.''

Mathias thought for a second. "It fits."

"Like a—" answered Washuta.

Suddenly, Mathias wheeled and dropped to the ground. He motioned for Washuta to do the same.

"What's up?" he whispered.

"I heard something." Mathias pointed up the slope.

Washuta scanned the terrain above them. A slight wind blew through the trees, but nothing else moved. "You sure?"

"I don't know," he shrugged. "It was too quick." He pointed to a low bank that rose up not far in front of them. A tree had blown down over it, and offered some good protection.

Washuta nodded. He set off for the bank so fast that a rooster tail of snow flew out behind. Mathias caught up to him, under the tree, and took a few breaths.

"I'm going to have another look," said Mathias. He peered out over the top edge. It was a mistake, but it was too late to do anything. He got nailed, square on the top of his helmet. He slid back under the tree.

"I'm hit," he said. "I think it's bad."

"Fatal," said Washuta. "Face it, dude. You took a high-velocity snowball at close range. There's just not much that we can do."

He leaned back against the bank. A couple of seconds later, Tyler and Devere slid over the edge. Crane dropped off of the tree. Mathias looked up at them and groaned.

Crane ignored him. "What's the deal on the tracks?" he asked.

"We sniffed them up and down," answered Washuta, "and the bird dogs report that they were made by the Soviet pilot after he ejected. He may still be in the area. We should assume that he has a radio and that perhaps he has already signaled for a pickup."

"But does he know where the plane is?" Crane asked.

"Unlikely," answered Washuta. "Where he came down and where the plane came down could be miles apart."

"All right," said Mathias. "We'll steer clear of him. Chances are that he just wants to get picked up and flown out. I don't think that he'll be a factor. Unless we've been spotted."

Tyler stood up. He was anxious to get moving. Washuta did some work with the maps. They had been on a north-south line and were reaching the end of the sector. It seemed pretty obvious. They had to work east.

Mathias spread them out and they set off.

Crane held down one end of the line. He and
Tyler took the other. The terrain got more
difficult. The land broke into a series of ra-
vines that cut down from the higher ground.
The trees were closer together. Crane got
the feeling that whatever they had been
on the edge of, they were getting into the
thick of it now.

Tyler, not thrilled with the deteriorating
landscape, wanted to talk.

"There's a better way to do this, Mathias.
I hope that you're aware of that."

"No." He pulled himself over a fallen
tree.

"Of course there is. Now the first thing is
to head south, go down to Algeria and set
up a base camp. We'll pick a spot not too far
from the water, stock up on vital fluids and
settle in. Then, we just wait for illegal arms
dealers to offer it to us. Then—"

Mathias extended his arm to hold Tyler
back. "Good idea, Tyler. Too bad we're just
not dressed for the weather."

After another half hour, Tyler spotted it.
Twenty feet across, a huge gash ripped
through the forest. Trees lay torn down,
pointing toward a blackened area of snow.

Mathias looked for the other guys. They
were down the slope, but even from that
distance they had spotted the crash site. He

caught Devere's attention, then signaled him to take the others over on the right. He wanted to be sure that there were no surprises hiding in the bushes.

He and Tyler closed in on the left. The snow was clean and the winds were calm. No one made a sound. They worked around the perimeter of the site. On the eastern edge, it opened up and they could see out across the valley. Once again, they were out in the open. This fact wasn't wasted on Tyler.

"I feel like I should wave," he said.

"Save it," whispered Mathias.

They circled around and met up with the other cadets about fifty yards past the plane.

"Nothing," said Devere.

"We're out in front on this one," said Tyler. "Everybody else is playing catch-up."

"Don't tempt them, Tyler," said Crane quickly.

"You worry too much, man."

"Only when you're around," Daryl said, moving off. "Let's see what we've got."

They approached the main section of the fuselage and cockpit. Devere looked at the wreckage. "The condition is good, for something that dropped out of the sky."

The wings had been sheared away from the body. Most of the tail section was gone. The rest of the plane was bent and twisted.

He slipped off his pack and started nosing around inside. Washuta joined him. Crane went to the other side and was soon just legs sticking out of the frame. The twenty-foot section of twisted metal was getting a good deal of attention.

Mathias gave them a few minutes to check out the situation. Then he asked Devere how it looked.

"Well, the port engine ripped off its mounts and was rammed about six feet forward. It twisted up the frame, and compressed everything in front. The space where the cockpit used to be is flattened into the nose. The impact jammed the nose aft about a yard and a half. No way anyone could have gotten to the box."

"Terrific," said Tyler. "We avoid the needle-in-the-haystack detail. Now what?"

"We cut."

Mathias looked at Devere. "How long?"

"An hour. Maybe two."

"Great. Let's get this thing open."

Devere took charge of the operation. He had the guys break out the equipment and lay it out along the left side of the fuselage. This was going to be different than any operation that he had done along the Gulf Coast, but the same principles would apply. Metal is metal. You work clean, you don't make stupid mistakes, and you make real sure that nothing heavy falls on your head.

A five-ton hydraulic jack was used to open some space between the wing mount and the central rib. This allowed Washuta to work back the skin and expose the struts. Fluid started to drip out of several lines. This caught everyone's attention, but according to Washuta, it was just from the hydraulics and wasn't flammable.

Devere was ready to start cutting with the portable acetylene torch they'd brought, but he held off. "How do you know it's not flammable?"

"It's standard wherever you go," Washuta answered. "All of our jets use the non-flammable fluids."

"This is not one of our jets," said Devere, making his point with a carbide saw in his hand. "And I don't want to find out the hard way."

No one moved. The fluid continued to drip. Then Tyler stepped forward. "This matter is easily settled," he said, reaching into his pocket. He pulled out a book of matches and lit one. A small pool of fluid had collected in a wrinkle of the metal skin.

Tyler looked at his buddies, raised his eyebrows, and dropped it in. The match flickered and the flame went out. Tyler stood back. "And that, gentlemen, is how that goes."

"You're a real Dr. Science," said Devere, swinging his leg back up to where he could work.

"More like a major jerk. The whole thing could've blown," Crane said.

"At least I took action—not like you guys from Wimp Point."

Crane grabbed Tyler and pushed him up against the metal hull.

Mathias jumped in between them. "Cool it, Crane. Now!" Crane slowly released Tyler and stepped aside. "Why don't you guys get the Russians to referee? I sure as hell don't have the time."

"Yo, Mathias. Listen up," Devere said suddenly.

Mathias turned and looked out over the valley. It was faint, but getting louder. It was the beating sound of a helicopter.

The other guys heard it and stopped moving. There were two choppers, about four miles out. They were working straight up the valley, one ridge over.

"Get close to the plane. Do it!" Mathias ordered. The cadets hunkered down close to the wreck, trying to blend in.

Thirty seconds later, the choppers faded over the hills and were gone. It had only taken that long, but now the game had changed.

FIVE

"I see it," yelled Devere. "The thing's right here."

He had burrowed four feet into the plane and his words had a strange echo to them.

"I've got it in my hand," he said. "It's attached through the bottom plate. There are some cables and stuff, but it's here."

Tyler climbed up to the top. Crane and Washuta worked from the bottom. Half a dozen hands pulled, cut and pried out enough space to clear out the box.

"Hey," called Devere, "take it easy."

Devere twisted over to get a better angle. His breathing was strained. Working upside down in such a cramped space wasn't easy.

But they were close now. This box was about to give itself up.

A bolt twisted free. "Now we're cooking," Devere called out. "One down and one more to go." He pressed a little further in. "How are you coming on those cables down there?"

"We're almost home," answered Washuta. "Just a little bit more."

Then from the nose of the plane, Mathias called out, "Don't cut those cables! Take your hands off that box." He ran back to Devere, leaned in and said, "Keep the box where it is. Don't move it around. This system is wired."

Devere pulled his hands off the data recorder like it just got hot.

"I hear you," said Washuta. "What's the problem?"

Mathias pushed his head into the wreckage. Through various cracks and openings, he could see at least part of everyone that was working. "System's connected to a self-destruct relay that's mounted up front. I don't know what the trigger mechanism consists of, but there's ten pounds of semi-solid explosives waiting to go off."

One by one, they pulled out of the plane. Mathias went forward to point out the explosives, which had been carefully molded into the insulation separating the forward cockpit wall and the electronic-relay control board.

Tyler looked right where Mathias was pointing, but he couldn't make out what exactly it was that they were looking at. Finally he had to ask, "Where are the explosives?"

"Right here," Mathias said. "The white stuff that looks like insulation."

"That?" Tyler asked.

"Sure," answered Mathias. "What did you expect, ten red sticks of dynamite taped together with a black detonator box on the side?"

"Something like that," he said, nodding his head. "But the thing is, it looks like it belongs in there. How do you know it's not really insulation?"

"Wait a second," said Devere, pointing straight at Tyler. "If he reaches for his pocket and pulls another stunt, I'm out of here."

"He could try it, but it wouldn't work. This type of explosive is simply too stable."

"Why don't we just take the stuff out and put it under a tree over there? As long as it doesn't get hit by lightning, we'll be fine. We can finish with the data box and catch a ride out."

"Taking it out could set it off," explained Mathias. "Depending on how it's been set up, there are a dozen ways to make it go.

With a manual, a wiring diagram, the test scopes, and about a month of free time, it could be doped out and disconnected. But out here, there's no way to do the job."

Devere shook his head. "We were that close," he said. "We did everything right and we got that close to bringing it on home." He slid down against the plane. He was irritated and it showed. He reached into his pocket for a chocolate bar and nearly tore it in half just getting past the wrapper.

Washuta dropped down beside him. Devere flipped him the broken half of the bar and said, "Here. These things make me sick."

Washuta took it in one bite. "Anyway, we did a good job of rip and strip inside the plane," he said.

"Yeah," said Devere, still chewing. He stuck out his hand and Washuta tapped it with his.

Tyler sat down alongside of Devere. "Seems like we should get a souvenir for our work."

"The U.S. Chop Shop Team could arrange it. Maybe a wing nut or something."

"Screw the wing nuts," said Crane. "We have a mission here. There's got to be a way at that box."

"All right, Crane," said Tyler. "You take the back and I'll take the front. We'll roll this plane down the hill."

"Yeah, right," said Mathias dryly. "It weighs too much. What we need is a tow truck."

Washuta jumped up and grabbed Mathias by the shoulders. "Radical! Why not call a tow truck?"

Devere slid his helmet down over his eyes. "Oh, no," he said sadly. "It's contagious."

Washuta ignored the comment. He went over to Crane. "We have a payload sitting here on the ground. We want the data box. It weighs about fifteen pounds. We can't remove it. I say we request an aircraft. Have them come in, strap onto the plane, and lift the whole thing right off this mountain."

It was a straightforward idea. He gave it a few seconds to sink in.

Mathias shook his head. "It's full of problems."

"Sure," said Washuta. "But at least from a technical standpoint, the plan could work."

Mathias nodded.

Washuta played it out. "The frigate *Orion* is probably only twenty miles off the coast of Norway. Like all the ships in its class, it's got a rescue chopper on the aft deck. If we can get the OK, they could be here in . . ." he paused to do some calculations, "less than thirty minutes. Figure another thirty minutes to coordinate the lift, and in under two hours, the box would be safe in international waters, on its way toward the Atlantic.''

"Can their equipment handle something like this?'' Tyler asked.

Washuta nodded. "The Stallion chopper runs off twin turbo shafts each with over four-thousand horsepower. It cruises at a hundred seventy miles per hour and can lift fifteen thousand pounds at sea level, probably twelve thousand pounds at this altitude. When it was in one piece, the fighter had an empty weight of . . .'' he paused to think it through, "let's say seventeen thousand pounds. Most of that would be from the power plants, which have been stripped off. Then there are the wings and the rest of it that are scattered around. All told, this part of the airframe goes about four tons. A Stallion could handle that load.''

"We'll have to break radio silence,'' Crane said. "That could let the Soviets know our position. If it takes the Stallion thirty minutes to get here, they might have to wait in line just to land.''

"I can send a pulse-code transmission,'' Mathias added. "If the frequencies are mixed together, it comes across like radio garbage.''

"Is it foolproof?'' asked Tyler.

"They'll never get the message,'' answered Mathias, "but there's a chance that they could lock onto part of it long enough to get a partial fix on our location. But, what about the payload? If Washuta's wrong about the Stallion, we end up with twice the problem that we have already."

"I can cut this crate down to make weight," Devere pointed out. "There's ten feet of tail section we could lose, no problem. That should knock off at least two tons."

Mathias turned to look at the horizon. It was his command decision. His responsibility. No way could they complete the mission under their present orders. Not since the choppers buzzed so close. It was risky, but the payoff was big.

Turning back to face the rest of the guys, he smiled and gave them the high sign.

"All right!" Washuta shouted.

Tyler shoved him. "We're using the radio, not your big mouth, man."

Everyone laughed.

"Okay, Devere. Take Big Mouth here and start cutting. Tyler, Crane, you're on watch. I'll get the message out. Let's move."

Devere fired up his torch and started his surgery. Washuta help him pry away the heated metal.

Mathias cracked open the radio gear. He connected the receiver, transmitter, encoder and frequency splitter together, then patched them into the power pack. He took off his helmet, pulled on the headset, and switched on the encoder drive. Within minutes the message was entered, scrambled, then transmitted in random pulses.

"How long before response time?" Tyler asked over his shoulder.

"Depends. Two minutes at this distance—once the decision is made."

Mathias knelt down next to the unit, watching for the LED lights that would indicate an incoming signal. The hiss of Devere's torch was the only sound.

Suddenly, the display light flickered.

"This is it," said Mathias.

The signal was automatically decoded and appeared on the screen.

STAND BY.

"What's the word?" Crane asked, turning.

"Standing by," answered Mathias.

"Sure," Tyler said. "Easy for them to say. We're the ones on the line."

"You got that right for once, Tyler," Crane agreed. "The brass always take their—"

Mathias held up his hand. Signal lights flashed across the radio. A moment later, a message appeared on the screen.

LIFT REQUEST DENIED. MISSION TO BE ABORTED. PROCEED FOR EXIT ON ORIGINAL TIME SCHEDULE. END.

"Damn!" said Mathias, punching the snow.

Hearing Mathias over his torch, Devere shut it off and looked up. Washuta dropped his jack and stood.

Crane and Tyler moved closer to Mathias.

"Clearance denied."

"Explanation?" Tyler asked.

Mathias shook his head.

"Command station, hell!" Crane said. "More like the U.S. Wimp Patrol."

"So, now what, chief? Pack up the ol' marbles and split?" Washuta was steaming.

"Looks that way, don't it, man?" Devere started packing.

"Hold up, Devere. I'm thinking," Tyler said.

"First time for everything."

Tyler ignored the comment. "The way I see it, it's hard to follow orders if you never receive them."

Mathias had thrown off his headset and stood with the rest of the cadets, listening to Tyler.

"Communications equipment gets damaged by midnight airdrops. Sometimes the receiver goes down in midmessage."

"Cute, Tyler," Mathias said. "But we still need a chopper to yank this junk back."

"And we just saw two fly past a few minutes ago," Washuta picked up the thread.

"You flight cadets are sure quick on the uptake." Tyler touched his head with his finger.

"Those were Soviet birds," Mathias answered.

"A minor detail. Nothing a little Russian accent can't fix, Komradsky." Tyler smiled and klicked his boots in the snow.

"Could work. The radio output would need to be low . . ." Mathias's mind was already working.

"No problem about me flying that bird. The Soviets ripped off all our specs."

"But what about the time factor?" Devere said. "No way we'll be able to cut the fat off the plane, steal the chopper, rig up and make the rendezvous."

"Devere's right, for a change," Tyler agreed. "And we can't blow our cover with radio contact."

The cadets stood silent for a minute. Then Crane spoke up.

"I got it! Overland courier!"

"Get real, Crane. What are we, the U.S. Mail?" Washuta barked.

"Listen, we need more time, right?"

"Right," Mathias agreed.

"Okay, we can't use the radio. The pickup point is only thirteen miles away. One man without gear could make it in three hours, tops. He meets the crew, does a song and dance about weather problems and gets another two hours. You guys fly in and we're heroes. I'll even volunteer."

Everything was coming together. The boys waited for Mathias to give the order.

"Hell," Mathias said, looking around, "they ordered us to execute this mission. It was their op plan that didn't respond to new field conditions, not ours. I say we take a little command initiative and take this sucker back—our way!"

SIX

About four miles east of the crash site, Mathias and Washuta were flattened out along the top of a ridge. Switching to infrared, they scanned the valley for a helicopter. Not only did they have a clear view of the land, but they were in line of sight with Tyler. He was about eighty yards down the slope, concealed at the edge of the tree line. He was set up with the radio and was ready to transmit on signal.

Mathias scanned the distant ridge lines. The Soviet search teams had passed up the valley twice in the last two hours. They had been predictable in their flight patterns. Mathias was counting on them to make one more run. They were set up and ready, and all they needed was the opportunity. It had better come pretty soon. A weather front had moved in from the coast, lowering the ceiling down to a few thousand feet.

"I think we got something," said Washuta. "It's at three o'clock, about two fingers above the rim, and it's flying north."

Mathias angled it off and tried to spot the target.

"You got it yet?" Washuta asked.

"Don't see a thing," answered Mathias.

"You have the eyesight of a worm." He nudged the binoculars about a quarter of an inch to the right; about fourteen miles on the horizon. Mathias nodded.

Washuta kept it in sight. "Looks like the only one," he said.

Mathias followed the flight line, checking for a second one. If they were working in pairs, the deal was off. They couldn't handle two of them. He saw only the one helicopter. If there was another one out there, it was flying lower and would be all but impossible to spot. He had to take that chance.

"This is it," he told Washuta. Then he flicked his flashlight twice.

This was the signal, this is what Tyler had been waiting for. He was the bait in this operation, and it was time for him to go to work. The radio was ready. Mathias had set the frequency and clipped it down to min-

imum output. This last modification had
been critical. It limited the transmission
range to under ten miles.

Tyler was ready to go on the air. He knew
almost thirty words in the mother tongue
of Russia, and he planned to use nearly
every one.

He flipped the switch, lifted the pause
and called out for assistance. He used a
husky voice to conceal his doubtful accent
and, just for extra measure, he rocked the
transmit button in and out of position. This
added some static, giving the impression
that the equipment was on its last legs.

The transmission lasted about eight seconds. Nothing came back to him, so he re-
peated the procedure. He needed to be on
the air long enough for the Soviet crew to
locate the point of transmission. Mathias
said it could take three or four tries, but
still, he didn't want to strike up a conversation with them. He just didn't have that
much to say.

As Tyler worked away with the foreign-
language show, Washuta and Mathias
moved into position. They saw the Soviet
helicopter change course and swing toward their location. It was still eight to ten
miles out, but it was riding this signal in.
They backed off the ridge and climbed
across the series of ledges that led down
to the clearing. They stopped by the edge,

about eight feet above the open ground. Tyler was about forty yards away inside the tree line.

The clearing was only fifty yards across at the widest point and broken into different levels by splits in the rock. This would make it difficult to bring in a helicopter and that, according to Washuta, was the whole idea.

From the other side of the ridge, they could hear the beat of the approaching helicopter. It was deep and smooth and grew steadily louder. Mathias took the gloves off of his hands and stuffed them into his pockets. He couldn't see, but knew he was ready.

The sound of the helicopter was close. Mathias swiveled around just in time to see it come over the ridge. The thing was huge, the size of a house. He could feel the vibration, from the air to his stomach and right into the rock. It was coming over low, just a hundred feet off the ground. The downblast from the main rotor whipped through the trees like a storm. It passed slowly overhead and hovered over the clearing. Then it began to turn to the left and follow the tree line around. Mathias couldn't see the pilot through the side window. He knew that the first officer would be seated alongside. Behind them, by the rescue hatch, would be the operations crew. Altogether, there could be three, four, or five on board.

The chopper had circled all the way around until it just passed their position. Then it stopped and held. Mathias flattened straight out on the ground. The arms and back of his jacket chattered in the down-blast. The powdery snow swirled up around him like a blizzard. He rolled his head back. He had no problem making out the arma-ment pod mounted under the nose. It was a three-piece turret with two rotary can-nons and a vertical-feed grenade launcher. If the right button got pushed, Mathias knew that he and this entire hillside would be history.

The helicopter dipped its nose and came forward. Mathias tucked his head under his arms. There was nothing else that he could do. For thirty seconds, it hung there, right in front of them. Then it rolled to the left and turned to face out across the clearing.

Mathias lifted his head. He couldn't be-lieve it. He could see why the helicopter had turned away from them. Tyler was crawling into the clearing. He was about ten feet out from the trees, dragging himself through the snow. His head was down, one arm limp at his side. He was holding a flash-light to guide the chopper. He made one more effort to go another few feet, then he slumped back into the snow and stopped moving.

The helicopter began to descend. Its seventy-foot rotor kicked out a cloud of snow a hundred feet in every direction. When it was still ten feet off the ground, Mathias jumped up. Washuta followed a second later. They leaped off the ledge and sprinted out into the clearing. All around them, the snow whipped through the air. They could barely see a thing. The rotors were still up to power when they reached the tail section. Washuta ducked under it to the left side and Mathias came up on the right.

Five feet forward, the hatch door opened. One of the crew waited on the edge as another one jumped down to the ground. Mathias dove past the opening, clipping the legs out from the first soldier. The second man lost balance, also, and the three of them ended up on the ground. Mathias was fast and clean. He spun back with a kick to the chest of the first crewman and came up on the second with a punch below the ribs. They dropped to the snow, looking for breath. The cadet took their sidearms, caught a foothold, and vaulted in through the hatch door.

The pilot was slumped off to the side holding his head. Washuta was at the controls and eased the engines down. Mathias

jumped back to the ground. He secured the
two crew members with plastic tie strips,
back to back. Washuta appeared in the
hatch, dragging the pilot. Already secured, he was lowered out and added to
the group.

Next came the crash kit. Washuta went
through it and removed the radio, flares,
and flashlights, and something that looked
like it could be eaten. The rest of the sur-
vival gear was lowered down. The crew
would have to spend the rest of the night
there. Without a signaling device, they
couldn't get picked up until the next day.
By then, it would long be over.

Washuta climbed back into the cockpit to
look things over. Mathias trotted across the
clearing to meet Tyler. He had gone back to
pack up the radio and was now carrying it
out.

"Let me help you with that stuff." He
slid his arm through a strap and lightened
Tyler's load by at least thirty pounds. They
hustled back to the helicopter. As they
passed the Soviet crew, Tyler started yelling in French. He went on for a few sen-
tences, then switched voices and answered
himself in Italian.

As they reached the hatch door, Mathias
boosted the equipment on board, put one
foot on the pylon, then turned to Tyler and
asked, "What was all that about?"

Tyler smiled. "Just some disinformation," he shouted over the engines. "This way, they won't know who to blame for ripping off their machine." They climbed inside. Washuta was at the controls. Tyler tossed the gear onto a side mount rack and then stepped forward into the cockpit.

"Is there a qualified co-pilot for this rig?" he yelled as he tapped on the empty flight seat.

Washuta shook his head.

"Good," answered Tyler. "I'll take the job." He settled into the seat, strapped in, and positioned his boots down among the hydraulic foot controls.

Washuta spotted this out of the corner of his eye and signaled him to put on the headset. "You might want to take it easy down there with those controls," he said into his mike. "Depending on which way you move them, you could either flip us over or blast a real big hole in that mountain over there."

"Whoa now, Mr. Washuta," said Tyler over the intercom, straightening up in his seat. "I'm here strictly as an observer." He looked over to the pilot. "You *do* know how to fly this thing?"

Washuta was trying to decide if one of the levers, clearly labeled in Russian, would control the trim or the lift. He kept this question to himself, but he did respond to

Tyler. "Of course I can fly this," he said casually. "Like I said before, they've got the same controls as we do. It's just getting the balance right between the power to the main rotor and the countertorque coming from the tail rotor."

"I see," said Tyler, yawning.

"Now, if you keep things balanced," Washuta continued, "everything is fine. But if you get too much tail . . ."

No such thing, thought Tyler.

". . . you'll flip over end for end. And too much main, you'll spin like a top."

Tyler shrugged. "It still beats walking," he said. "Especially when you can't see anything."

The only light in the cockpit was a faint glow from the gauges, meters, displays, and dials that were spread out below the windscreen. They were all illuminated with the same red light.

When Mathias slapped his shoulder, Washuta was ready. He turned up the power, and the twin turbines started to wail. He checked the RPM and tweaked it some more. The tail came up, the frame trembled, and then the whole thing pulled free of the ground. They started to rotate left, but Washuta evened it out. They climbed to one thousand feet in minutes, then circled to the southwest. They were free and clear.

Washuta tilted his head back. "We did it, Sonny Boy. We pulled it right out from under their feet." He smacked his lips like he had just finished a meal. "You should have been there, it was first rate prime."

"We're barely clear of the treetops," Tyler said, "and this one is already telling stories like we just made history."

"And that's just how it was," Washuta said, smiling. "The three of us, swooping down out of the blue, twisting and diving. . . ."

"Excuse me, Mr. Washuta," Tyler broke in, "but I was the one crawling through the damned snow. There was not a lot of swooping involved."

Suddenly, a flash of blinding light burst into the cockpit. Washuta banked hard to the right and powered up fast.

"Where in the hell did that come from?" he yelled out.

Tyler was against the windscreen. Mathias had slid back to the hatch. He was the one who saw it first.

"Soviet chopper," he called out. "She's off the port beam and down below."

"Damn," said Washuta. "We better split." He pulled a tight-radius turn and kept on climbing. The searchlight caught them again, but this time it was just for a second. They were moving fast.

Mathias had been leaning out the door,

trying to keep the other chopper in view. Something was wrong. He pulled inside and yelled forward.

"Back it off! You're just going to make them nervous. They didn't know what happened. They think we're just another one of their units."

Washuta eased off. "Could be," he said. He checked through the side screen that went down to floor level. Through it, you could see almost straight down, and there was the other chopper, riding smooth and easy. Then it became obvious. He'd turned off the ship-to-ship frequency, so when this other chopper tried to raise them on the radio, they couldn't get through.

Tyler clicked in. "They're not trying to shoot us down," he said. "We better play along with them, at least for now."

Washuta nodded. He eased down in a slow and respectable way. As he was sliding up alongside the other chopper, it pulled away and headed east.

"Stay with him," said Mathias, putting on his headset. "Just like we're going home together."

"That's all right," said Washuta. "We'll just tag along a ways and then we'll give them the slip."

Tyler wasn't convinced. "Mathias," he yelled, "you're just dreaming." He pointed out the array of instruments spread across the cockpit: infrared, heat-seeking, radar-guided laser weapons. He shook his head and looked out the side window. "Look at their stuff. We can't just disappear."

Mathias shook him off, saying, "Ask Washuta, boy pilot."

Tyler looked at Washuta. He tried to keep a serious face, but it didn't last long. "Yeah, right."

"Get stuffed, Tyler," Washuta answered.

They had climbed to twenty-five hundred feet. The Soviet helicopter stayed out in front, its red tail strobe flashing out its position. Their air speed was steady at 140 knots. They had covered seventeen miles.

Mathias took a look at the chart. If they held steady on course and speed, in about six minutes they would cross into Soviet air space. He pointed this out to Washuta.

"If we pull out now, they'll see it for sure."

"Can't we slip off their radar screen," asked Mathias, "by diving up one of these valleys?"

"Negative," answered Washuta. "They've got the altitude and could trace us all the way to the ground if necessary."

Tyler nodded. He looked out the right side, and his eyes went wide. "Mayday! Mayday!" he yelled.

"Where?" asked Washuta, bending forward to see.

Tyler was pressed against the plexi. "Two more choppers," he said, "coming up starboard side."

Washuta caught their lights. One was nearly a beam, about two hundred yards out. The second was further back. He checked the radar screen. He hadn't been watching it closely, and now he knew that it was a mistake. All told, he counted seven aircraft within a ten-mile radius. Four of them, including their own, were clustered together. Three more were coming in from the south.

"Getting crowded," he said.

"We've just crossed over," said Mathias. "We're in Soviet territory now."

"Looks the same," said Tyler, who had taken on the duties of primary aircraft spotter.

The lead Soviet chopper turned south and started to descend. Washuta held back slightly until he was last in line of the four aircraft. They were down to one thousand feet. The ground below them was dark and open.

Stretched out in front of him, Washuta followed the flashing line of strobes. The other three from the south had come into view. "This is a good place to skip out," said Washuta. "Tighten up your belts. I don't want anyone flying out the window."

Tyler took a deep breath and pulled in the strap on his seat harness. Mathias took the engineer's seat and strapped himself down.

They had dropped to five hundred feet and were cutting across a valley. Their airspeed hung at 140 knots. The chopper group rose up the far side and went over the top like they were tied together.

Washuta tried to whistle, but his mouth had gone dry.

Spread out before them was a Soviet base. It was lit up from end to end and jumping with activity. They followed the other choppers in on the approach. As they crossed over the base, they could see the temporary crew shelters, support vehicles, communication tower, and the supply trucks entering off the road to the east.

There was no airstrip, but at one end a landing zone had been laid out and marked with green lights. The choppers in front started to go in, but Washuta hung back until he was last in line. He waited until the last chopper touched down, then proceded out over the eastern perimeter and held a steady line until the camp was out of sight. Washuta banked to the north, dropped the nose and took them right down toward the ground. He kept their altitude low and their speed up as they rolled west over the terrain.

Phase one was complete. They had a chopper.

SEVEN

The steady drone of the helicopter beat through the air. Devere heard them coming in. At least he thought it was them, but he was so tired that it almost didn't matter.

He had single-handedly broken the air-frame down. He had trimmed off ten feet aft of the cockpit and burned out the landing struts that had still been folded up in the wells. That made the package smaller and lighter. Then he isolated the lift points on the lower half of the frame and checked them to determine that they were sound.

He could see them now. They were up over the trees. He trotted out toward the middle of the open ground. From inside his jacket he pulled a flashlight. It was all he had to guide them in. He switched it on and nothing happened. A rough shake got it to work. The chopper had gone wide to the left. Still, the light must have helped because they straightened out and came in on line.

Devere braced himself. They were seventy feet up and the noise of the engines could be felt right in his stomach. The downblast kicked up the snow so violently that he had to protect his eyes with the back of his arm. He didn't even see them land. When the power was cut and the rotors slowed, he hustled out to meet them.

The hatch door opened and Mathias jumped out.

" 'Bout time you got back," Devere said, smiling.

"Yeah, we did all right," Mathias admitted.

"All right?" Washuta said proudly, as he appeared in the doorway. "This thing is as awesome as they come." He sat down on the edge of the hatch. "Seventy feet long with a six-blade main rotor that runs off two turbo shafts putting out eight-thousand horsepower. We've had her up to one hundred ninety-six miles an hour and the fuel tanks are still half-full."

Tyler leaned out of the hatch. "And," he said, "it's got factory-installed air conditioning."

Tyler and Washuta jumped down to the ground. They trailed Devere, who was on an inspection tour of the Soviet chopper. He was walking aft, alongside the gray and green fuselage. He ducked under the wing pylon where the extended tanks were mounted and had a look at the reinforced bridging that ran under the belly. The heavy winches were mounted to the topside of this framework, and the rigging hung down below.

Behind this, the fuselage narrowed and swept up into the tail section. This ended in a single stub wing on one side, and the tail rotor on the other. The unit badges were up there, too. They were stenciled on in bright white paint, a split-image star with yellow bands running completely around the tail.

Devere took a few steps back. He looked from one end of the helicopter to the other and said, "You guys scalped a major piece of equipment here. Must be worth fifty million."

"More than that," said Tyler, casually leaning on the rocket rack. "Don't forget, you have to add in tax and dealer prep. And then there's license and insurance fees. It really does add up. And just to go for a test ride. . . ."

"Tyler!" Mathias called out. "Put a cork on it. We're only borrowing this, not buying it." He turned to Devere. "How's the cargo?" he asked.

"Ready to go. All we have to do is lay out the cables."

"All right," said Mathias. "Let's sort it out."

Washuta stepped forward. "In a regular lift operation, the helicopter flies over the payload and drops the cables for the ground crew to hook up. We're going to have trouble doing it that way because . . ."

"We don't have a ground crew," answered Tyler. "Everybody's got to be up in the chopper, or else they miss the ride out."

"Unless they hook onto the frame and then ride up in the sling," corrected Washuta.

"No problem," said Devere. "And better me than anybody else." He waved his hand confidently, his eyes bright. "I've got the time in."

"You're elected." Mathias looked at his watch. "Crane should have made pickup an hour ago."

Devere nodded. "We need that delay."

"He'll get it." Mathias boosted himself up through the hatch door. Tyler followed him.

"Hey, slick," Devere called out.

Tyler held the edge of the doorframe and looked back out.

"You talking to me?" he asked sharply.

"Yeah," answered Devere. "Don't forget to lower the sling on signal. I don't want to hear how it slipped your mind."

Tyler waved him off. Washuta fired up the engines and waited for all the systems to come up to level. Devere crouched quickly and trotted back to the wrecked frame.

The engines on the helicopter came up to full power. It slowly rose off the ground, went over the tree line at the end of the clearing, and climbed to two hundred feet. It circled back around and hovered over the plane. The spotlight mounted on the belly switched on, and the ground was flooded in light.

Looking up, Devere couldn't see the chopper in the glare behind the white spot. The twin steel cables were visible as they came down. The oiled strands glistened against the dark. He held his left arm straight out and waved his right hand in toward his chest. The cables were drifting wide. They shifted back over the frame. Devere positioned himself under the aft line. The hook dropped down into his reach. Ten more feet, and he had enough slack to maneuver. He pulled the line over the top of the fuselage and snaked it into place. He looped it through and fastened it with a snap clamp. One line was secure.

While Washuta was working hard to hold

things steady, Devere scrambled for the
other line. The end was lying limp on the
ground. He picked it up and pulled it around
to the right side. Then the slack went out.
The rear cable tightened up and the airframe shifted over. Devere lost his balance
and slipped. He scrambled to his feet and
secured the cables. The load was ready.

From twenty feet back it looked good. The
sling was down and ready to go. He climbed
in and cinched up the straps. Then he waved
his right arm in a circle and the line started
to reel up. He rode with the winch up at
ninety feet a minute.

The belly of the helicopter was about
twenty feet above him, but the noise and
the rotor blast made it seem like he was already riding the outside wing.

He pulled up past the hatch door. Mathias
and Tyler were both there. They reached
out for him. They were yelling something
but he couldn't hear. He was swung inside.
The winch was reversed, and they un-
hitched the sling and stowed it over the
swing arm.

"We all clear back there?" Washuta called
over the intercom.

"Ready to roll, skipper," shouted Devere,
giving him the thumbs up.

Washuta feathered the power to take the
slack out of the cables. The jolt shook the
helicopter. They rebounded, and took it up

again. This time he held it tight and for a few seconds they felt stretched out between the ground and the top nut of the rotor. Then he turned up the power and they rose free.

The crew cut loose in a wild victory shout. They all felt good. Phase two was complete. Tyler reassumed his position as co-pilot. Mathias breathed a visible sigh of relief and collapsed into a side seat. Devere took the one opposite him. He stretched out his legs and closed his eyes. There was no way that he was going to sleep through this, but that didn't mean that he wasn't going to try.

Washuta climbed to five hundred feet and headed south. The rendezvous had been set with a Sea Otter that would have landed a few hours ago. If Crane had convinced the crew to wait around for a while, there would be no problem. Washuta corrected his course a few degrees, then he asked Tyler to double check the chart for distance and heading.

"Aye, aye, skipper," Tyler answered cheerfully. He spread out the map and started to scrutinize. He called out some information that jibed with the current readings and Washuta accepted the facts, letting him know that here was hope for him on the flight deck—if he could learn to fly without getting sick.

Fifteen minutes into the flight, Washuta clicked in.

"This is the captain speaking. I don't mean to break in like this, but we're approaching PZ, boys. Unless we get some assistance on the flight deck, we might overfly our target. We are looking for an eighteen-seat, twin-engine Sea Otter. Thank you for your cooperation."

"You've got a solid-gold bedside manner," Tyler said. "Too bad it's wasted on this crew."

Washuta shrugged. "They may not look like much, but they're all we got."

Washuta descended to three hundred feet, lowering the airframe to seventy feet above ground. From their altitude, the terrain below looked like an even expanse of dark carpet, but was actually solid forest.

A split opened up in the land below them. It ran across their course and got wider as they approached. This was the river. It was frozen over and covered with snow. As they flew overhead, Washuta did a slow turn and followed it west. He dropped another fifty feet in altitude. That was as close as he could get.

He got to within fifty yards of the tree line and straightened out on a parallel course. Their airspeed was down to under sixty knots. If the plane was tucked away and covered over, it would be easy to miss.

Suddenly, Washuta saw the problem. It had been a mental error, an omission that had slipped into the plan. It was his responsibility and he knew it. He should have arranged for an identifying signal. Something that would let the crew on the ground know that they weren't a Soviet unit.

"Fire up the searchlight," Washuta said to Tyler. "We need it over on the left bank."

Tyler adjusted the hydraulic linkage and activated the bright spot. The light flared out over the snow, clear back to the tree line. No way that they could miss the plane now. A mile upriver, Tyler spotted it in a cove on the bank. Washuta slowed the speed, and held for a second. No one said anything. There wasn't any need. Pulled in tight against the trees, the Sea Otter waited. Tyler moved the light over the plane and the shadows shifted behind it. No one was in sight. The windows were blacked out. From what they could see, it looked deserted.

"Take us down," Mathias clicked.

Washuta swung the nose around and moved in toward the plane, carefully avoiding the trees. He settled down slowly until the Soviet plane they carried beneath them rested firmly on the snow.

Devere was already back at the hatch door and as soon as they stabilized, he was lowered out on the sling. He swayed slowly to the ground, but once his feet hit he was

on the go. He scrambled over the frame, re-
leasing the clamps and freeing the cables.
When everything was clear, he waved his
arms to the side, then took them straight up.
The cables reeled in and the helicopter
pulled back. Washuta circled away from the
trees and set down on the river. Tyler and
Mathias jumped out and ran low over the ice
to Devere's position.

"Not much of a welcome," said Tyler,
slightly out of breath.

They were alongside the wrecked fighter.
The twin-engine Otter was only fifty yards,
but there was still no sign of the crew.

Mathias motioned Devere to swing around
behind the plane and approach from the
trees. They gave him a minute to get into
position, and sprinted over to the plane.
They ducked around the forward wheel and
worked their way back to the wing. Mathias
motioned Tyler to hold steady.

They were just below the forward door. It
was closed and it looked sealed. The access
panel was alongside. Mathias opened it up
and released the locking mechanism. The
crew door popped open about an inch. He
reached up and pulled it down. It opened up
into three steps. The interior looked dark.

He eyed Tyler and grabbed the rail, swung
up onto the middle step, and dove through
the doorway. Tyler followed. They collided

into a body. Mathias saw a rifle and went for it with both hands.

"Freeze!" The command rang out from the front of the plane. The battery lights came on bathing the interior of the plane in a soft yellow light.

Mathias looked out from under the arms and legs that were tangled around him. Down the aisle, a black assault rifle was leveled his way. Crouched behind it was a man wearing a dark watch cap and a padded red jacket. He motioned for the cadets to raise their arms and move apart.

The other man got up and retrieved his rifle from the floor. He walked slowly over to Mathias, paused a minute to stare directly into his eyes, then lifted the rifle butt.

"Stow it, Williams," the first man ordered. The man backed off. "Either one of you hotshots named Mathias?"

Tyler looked up. "Yeah, we got a Mathias here. If you asked sooner, you could have saved your girl friend here some trouble."

Tyler started forward when the watch cap shifted the attention of his weapon saying, "Don't get anxious, punk."

Tyler relaxed, but the look on his face stayed just as hard.

"I'm Mathias. You can put down the weapons now. We are all part of the same operation."

But the man stayed wired. "Why the foreign chopper?" he asked.

"We don't like to walk," Tyler barked out.

"Cool off, Tyler. That's an order." Mathias turned toward the watch cap. "We stole it for transport."

"Where's the rest of your crew?" the man asked.

"Two more outside. Where's Crane?"

The watch cap slipped his rifle to the side and sat heavily into one of the seats. "Name's Anderson," he said. "We were contracted to fly five men out. That's all I know." He glanced between the boys. "There's been some activity around here, so when you dropped in with a Soviet chopper, we had to take precautions."

He hesitated for a second, then said, "That guy Crane never got here. He came close, but he didn't make it."

Tyler heard that and was ready to jump, but Mathias grabbed him.

Anderson continued. "We landed about an hour ago. We backed in here out of the way, to wait. About twenty minutes pass and there's some activity on the north bank. We check it out through the scopes. There's a patrol of a dozen men coming out from the trees. They head off to the east, keeping close to the cover. We know that the deal is bent because we're looking to fly out five guys, not twelve. So, we go up to the point for a better line of sight. We see one man toward the back of the patrol. His uniform was gray and white camo, such as you two are wearing. We keep them in sight as long as we can. About a mile upriver, a motorized patrol shows up from the east, they hook up with the first group and then head back. Since then, we've been waiting for you guys to show. So now we can take off.''

Tyler hit the flash point. "You just let him go like that? You just watch him from a distance until he's out of sight?''

Mathias backed him up against the wall, but Tyler wouldn't shut up.

"You're so quick to pull your weapons on us, but you sit on them sideways when it counts.''

"Listen, sonny,'' Anderson shot back, "if we committed ourselves to that type of response and we got nailed ourselves, the bottom would have been ripped out of the rest of the operation.''

"I thought you didn't know what the op was about,'' Tyler said bitterly, "that you were contracted to fly us out, nothing more, nothing less.'' His voice faded away. He was breathing hard. Mathias eased up. Tyler pushed his way out of the plane.

"There's a big piece of aluminum sitting out there in the snow,'' Mathias said.

"Winch it into the hold and fly it out instead of us. We're not ready to go." He walked out.

Anderson didn't say a word.

EIGHT

Vashuta had them skimming along just thirty feet off of the ice at better than a hundred miles an hour. Their course was simple, holding straight up the river. They were going after Crane.

How much had the Soviets pieced together? There was a Soviet helicopter crew camped out on the mountaintop. As soon as they were picked up, there would be no more mystery concerning their missing chopper.

Mathias let the details slide. They didn't matter that much. Not really. There was only one thing that was important here, and they were doing that right now. Rescuing Crane.

The Soviet patrol probably took several
hours to cover this ground and Washuta was
doing it in a matter of minutes. Their trail
was not hard to follow. The tracked vehicles
that they used chewed a sharp double line
up the length of the river. They'd catch the
patrol. What they'd do once they caught
them was another story.

They had covered almost twenty miles
and Washuta was becoming anxious. In a
few minutes they would be approaching the
border. If the patrol had already crossed
over, it might be too late to try anything.
They would have to turn back, and that
wasn't something that he wanted to con-
sider.

"That's it," yelled Tyler.

They were moving too fast. In seconds
the patrol was a mile behind them.

"Hold your course," Mathias clicked in
"but cut the speed as much as you can."

Washuta nodded. "They came out of nowhere," he said, easing off the power.

"That's the problem. It happened so fast
that we couldn't see anything. We'll have to
go back for a second look—on foot."

"We're not that far away," said Washuta
"If I set down, they'll hear the change and
they'll know that something is up."

"You don't have to stop," Tyler said
"Just swing down close and we'll jump out
the door."

Washuta looked at him. "Are you serious?"

"He's serious," answered Mathias.

"Sure, like rolling out of bed," said Tyler. "It's that easy." He swung out of the co-pilot's seat and squeezed out of the cockpit. Mathias followed him back to the hatch. Devere had it open.

Washuta angled down to less than twenty feet. Devere braced himself at the door, then eased out onto the wing pylon. The six-bladed main rotor was working right over his head, but he ignored it, got to the edge of the pylon and jumped.

He hit the ground, curled into a ball, and went over two or three times, fast and hard, until he came to a stop.

Mathias and Tyler had landed about twenty yards back and were up and moving toward him. Mathias took the lead and moved them out at a trot. They hung close to the edge, sometimes right under the trees. They moved quickly. Every few minutes Mathias would hold up his hand, stop, and listen. But there was only silence.

"A patrol doesn't disappear," said Mathias in a low voice. He pointed off to the right. "We'll work along parallel to the river," he said, "but farther back in the trees. They are out there. Watch where you walk. We don't want any more surprises."

They moved back into the trees, going slowly and carefully.

Tyler froze in place, and when they saw him, Mathias and Devere did the same. At first, the voices were quiet. They could be heard, drifting in and out, different voices in conversation. It was hard to tell how far off they were. It could be ten yards, it could be a hundred. Mathias was going to find out.

The land rose up slightly as he led the way. As they approached the bend to the right side, they knew they were getting close. They worked down to the edge. The river was thirty or forty feet below them and tucked in against the bank was the patrol. They had four tracked trucks and one open-backed snow cat. The men had broken out their gear and set up for the night. They had picked a good spot. They were out of the wind and nearly out of sight.

There was, however, no sign of Crane. The three of them kept watch for a solid fifteen minutes. They didn't even pause to blink. If he was down there, he was under wraps, hidden away in one of the trucks. He wasn't out in the open and socializing with the crew.

The three of them slid back from the edge.

"You think this might be a different patrol?" asked Tyler.

"Hard to say," answered Mathias. "It's in the right place and it seems to fit the de-

scription of the one that picked up Crane.
But from up here, we can't be certain."

"Let's cut through all of this," said Devere. "How many of us are going in to check
it out?"

Mathias looked at the two guys who were
at his side and said, "Just me."

Tyler began to open his mouth, but Mathias shut him down. "We're already over
the line on this." His voice was a hoarse
whisper, but carried a lot of weight. "We've
lost Crane and I'm not going to risk anybody
else. If I get stuck down there, both of you
pull out and hustle your butts back to Washuta. When I drop over this edge, that's it.
That's a direct order."

Devere stared at him for a second, then
looked away. The muscles in his jaw were
working back and forth. He didn't appreciate being cut down like that.

Devere hesitated, then said, "Don't screw
up."

"Thanks," said Mathias. He pushed himself up into a crouch, then added, "I never
learned how. That's how I got here."

"So much for the system of reward and
punishment," said Tyler.

Mathias ignored the comment. "Give me
fifteen minutes," he said, "then you're
outta here."

He rolled away from the other two, came
up behind a tree and stood up. He looked

down at the river. He was forty feet above the river and from where he was, it was almost straight down. There were three or four ledges between the top and the bottom that had been blown free of snow. The patrol was set up about sixty yards further up. He checked to see if they had any guards posted, but it didn't look like they made the effort. This meant either a sloppy operation or a skillful trap.

Mathias knew that there was only one way to find out. He slid over the edge and started to climb down, one hand at a time, one foot always in place. He moved like a spider. He didn't look down. Everything that concerned him was only an arm's reach away.

Halfway down he paused on a ledge. He crouched down to make himself small. He looked around to see if he was drawing a crowd, but everything was quiet. He resumed his descent. As he approached the bottom, the slope leveled out and he picked his way through the broken rock.

He worked his way closer. A light flickered behind one of the trucks. It caught his eye like a beacon and he froze in place. It only lasted for a second, then it went out. It was probably a cigarette. Mathias knew he would have to be careful.

He eased over the rocks and got to within ten yards of the first vehicle. From there on, it was open ground. He was tempted to cover that distance on the run, but he decided against it. The snow was too crusty. It would make too much noise. He would have to do it in style.

Crane stood up, dusted the snow off of his trousers, and tucked his hands into his jacket pockets. He walked from the edge of the riverbank out to the first truck like he owned the outfit. But as soon as he was within arm's length, he dropped to the ground and rolled under the truck.

He looked out from in between the track links. Most of the activity was at the other end of the camp, where the shelters were set up. He pulled himself out from between the tracks and took a quick look into the back of the truck. There were a few supply bags, but nothing else. He slid alongside the truck and crossed over to the next one in line. No sign of Crane.

He was moving toward the back of the next truck when he heard someone coming. Two soldiers came around the back. He lowered his head and turned face-in toward the front tire of the truck, as if he were taking care of some very ordinary repair. They passed right by. He took a quick look in the back and then moved to the last one.

It was parked the other way around, with the cab pointing out toward the river and the back facing the rest of the camp. He slid under the front of the truck and worked his way down. He crawled out and was halfway up when he heard voices. Without hesitation, Mathias hooked an arm over the tailgate, kicked his leg up and rolled into the back of the truck. He flattened out against the metal bed.

Mathias waited for them to pass, but they didn't. They were right outside, leaning against the outside of the truck. Their conversation grew louder by the minute. Then one speaker called out across the camp and a third soldier came over.

Mathias felt trapped. He couldn't move. He could barely breathe because the clouds of vapor would give him away.

The side of Mathias's face was flat against the bottom of the truck bed. He turned it slightly, and brushed a balled-up wrapper with his nose. He recognized the smell of stale chocolate—the same as the candy bars in their rations.

Mathias wanted to leap onto the roof and yell out so that Tyler and Devere would know. They had been right. Crane was in this camp somewhere. But he had to wait until those three soldiers leaning on his truck packed it in for the night before he could find him. He had been in the camp for nearly thirty minutes, maybe more. The longer he stayed, the more likely it became that he would get caught.

From the far end of the camp came other voices. A lone wolf howled. He sounded far away, but a few minutes later, he howled again. This time it was closer. There was a stir of activity from across the camp, shouting and some people running along the river. A moment later, shots rang out. There were four or five rounds. The three soldiers outside the truck were drawn into the commotion.

Mathias leaped over the tailgate and landed in a half crouch on the ground. For a split second, he froze, looking in all directions at once. There was no one between him and the riverbank.

He sprinted for the trees.

NINE

Washuta had been waiting for over three hours. He had landed the helicopter about two miles up the river. It was in the middle of nowhere. After a while, he started to believe that he was the last one of them still free. Crane was gone. And now the other three were long overdue. They shouldn't have worked it this way, but it was too late to go back.

He stretched out to get some sleep. It had been a while, and it felt good. He propped his legs up on a supply kit and tried to forget about the world. If no one showed by daybreak, he would have to face the facts.

He drifted in and out of sleep. He replayed parts of the operation. He saw the rest of them, they were back at the weather station chowing down to a steak dinner. They were talking. It was quite a party. At one point he heard someone say, "Mr. Washuta, please open the door."

He knew that it was part of the celebration, and that they were about to make a grand entrance. The reception was ready. The people were waiting. The food was hot. Again the announcement was made.

"The door, Washuta!"

He woke up quickly. It was still dark. He was in the helicopter and directly across from him was the hatch door. It was being pulled open. He scrambled to his feet and picked up a supply crate, pressing up against the near side of the wall. He was ready to do damage, just as soon as something moved.

The hatch opened and Tyler poked his head inside.

"Sleeping on watch, Cadet?" he asked.

Tyler climbed into the aircraft. Devere and Mathias followed him in. They dropped into various seats and propped their feet up where they could. Washuta lowered the supply tin.

"So what happened?" he asked. "Did you find the patrol? Was Crane there?"

"We are hot on the trail," said Tyler triumphantly. "It's only a matter of time."

"We didn't see Crane," Mathias explained, "but we checked out the patrol."

"And he escaped!" Washuta said, rolling his head down and slapping his leg. "I knew it! They tried, but he was too much for them."

Mathias shook his head. "Negative, bud."

Washuta looked up at Mathias. "How do you know?"

"Because there was no search activity, the patrol was quiet."

"The way that we see it," said Tyler, "the patrol grunts picked up Crane, held him for a while, maybe questioned him. But before long, they sent him on to higher ground."

"Then he's not in the area anymore. The guy could be anyplace."

"Maybe," said Tyler. "But the military's the same everywhere. When this patrol passes on Crane to the next rung up on the ladder in this sector, we figure it's got to be at the base."

"Great," Washuta said. "I'll call ahead for clearance so we can fly in and out like TWA."

"Something like that," Mathias said, yawning. "If Crane is at the camp, it won't be for long, so we'll have to hustle. The plan is that you fly low, out of their radar scan, and drop us off two miles from the perimeter. Tyler, Devere and I go in, grab our man and split. Clean and fast.''

"And what if you guys get caught?''

"That's not an option. Let's get going.''

Devere headed back to man the door. Mathias resumed his position as engineer.

"I'm getting to like this co-pilot job,'' Tyler joked, heading for the cockpit.

Washuta squeezed past him. "It's easy if you don't do anything.''

"Hey, at least I don't do anything *wrong.*'' He tilted his head back and called out to the engineer. "Tell him about our great escape.''

Mathias started to chuckle. Washuta looked back. "All you really need to know is that it came down to Tyler here barking like a dog.''

"Say what?'' Washuta said, adjusting his headset.

"Not a dog,'' Tyler clicked in, "a wolf. Man, I was so convincing, I even got shot at.'' He showed Washuta a hole in the side of his jacket.

"Too bad he wasn't wearing it at the time,'' Mathias laughed.

"You shoulda seen those Ruskies scramble. And in all the confusion, Mathias here managed to get out of the camp right under their noses. Citation material, if I say so myself.''

Washuta didn't look at all convinced and

responded by switching on the power. He checked down the systems. When things looked right, he pulled them back and they took off. They climbed over the trees and angled away from the river. They flew north about twenty miles before banking east. Washuta was fairly certain about the location. Tyler devoted his attention to the radar screen. Mathias worked out the plan in his hand. He tried to remember the details of the camp, the security at the perimeter, the placement of the buildings, the location of the landing zone. He didn't recall a radio tower or even a radar setup, though he knew that both had to be there.

"ETA, three minutes," Washuta announced. "I'll put you down nice and easy."

Mathias tapped Tyler, and they headed back to the door.

Devere had already opened it. He held onto the tie bar, looking for the base lights. He pointed to the east.

Mathias nodded, and grabbed the radio.

Washuta slowed speed and headed for a spot just outside a stand of trees, between them and the base. As soon as the wheels touched the snow, Devere, Mathias, and Tyler hit the ground, running straight for the camp.

Luckily, when the Soviets cleared out the temporary camp, their bulldozers had left

ten-foot mounds of snow around the perimeter. In the darkness, the cadets used them
for cover on their approach.

The main building and barracks shed
deep shadows under the high-pole mounted
lights placed around the camp. There was
no exterior fence, and the monitoring posts
were widely spaced. The base had one road
access.

With Mathias in the lead, the team moved
from mound to mound, until they were
close enough to sprint to the backside of
something that looked like an equipment
shed. Careful to remain completely in
shadow, they worked their way to a fuel
truck some ten yards from the main entrance.

Suddenly, they heard a chopper coming
in. It flew over the east side of the camp
and set down. Right away, a black car that
had been parked along the landing zone
pulled out and drove alongside the helicopter. A detail of soldiers approached the
main building. Two trucks and another car
pulled up behind them. Out of the car
stepped three civilians. They hustled into
the main building and the guarded doors
closed behind them.

After a few minutes, the guards opened
the doors. A detail of a dozen men came
out. They headed straight for the car in
front. A cluster of people, some in uni-

forms, some not surrounded it. From the middle of this, a young man in a camo flight suit was escorted to the rear door of the car. One of the soldiers lowered his head and pushed him inside.

"Did you see that?" whispered Tyler. His voice was hoarse with excitement. "It was Crane."

"Okay, now's our chance," Mathias whispered, pointing toward the open-back truck nearest to them. "Now."

The cadets covered thirty-odd feet in no time flat and hopped into the truck. They hid behind two large storage crates toward the back of the bed and waited. Tyler listened closely to the voices.

"I think they're taking him to another command location. Sounds close. Something about warm fires and vodka." Tyler smiled.

The truck door slammed and the engines started up.

Mathias nodded. "I hope we're going their way."

About an hour later, they felt the truck slow down. Tyler picked up some checkpoint exchanges between the driver and a sentry.

"Sounds like this is where we get off," he said.

As soon as the truck geared up, Devere moved toward the opening on his belly and looked out. They had passed an old stone-fence gateway and were headed toward a forest. He waved the other cadets forward. Just as the truck entered the trees, they jumped and ran for cover.

"I'm sick of snow," Tyler whined, dusting himself off behind a large hemlock tree.

"No time for complaints," Mathias said, watching the convoy. "We've got to stick close to Crane."

The trucks slowed down to negotiate the steep, snow-covered road and the cadets had no trouble following them. About two miles up the slope, the trees broke onto a large clearing.

Devere was the first to see the lights. "Man, will you look at that."

In the center of the snow stood a two-story stone hunting lodge. It had a high-pitched roof, two side wings and what looked like a stable and barn to the back. The only lights were in the large bay window on the first floor. There were soldiers stationed at twenty-foot intervals around the perimeter. The convoy stopped at the front door.

"Not bad for the starving masses. Soviet brass know how to live."

Mathias ignored Tyler's remark. "Devere, you and me find Crane. Tyler, you hang back with the radio. When you spot us, signal Washuta. He'll find us. Okay, let's hit it.''

TEN

Devere took the lead, moving between the trees quickly. Mathias kept his eyes on the guards. The two at the front walk never seemed to move. They were planted three paces down from the entrance and looked frozen in place. A dusting of snow had accumulated on the shoulders of their uniforms.

At the right end of the lodge was a covered terrace that projected from the building. A guard was posted there, as well. He paced back and forth through the shadows. On occasion, he leaned over the railing and attempted to check along the side of the lodge.

They circled around to the back of the lodge. From their position, the ground rose

up, providing some cover along the slope.
Mathias noticed there was no guard near the
large stone chimney. They sprinted up the
hill twenty yards to the base of the lodge,
then flattened out against the foundation to
the right of the chimney.

Devere watched the wall to the left and
the right as Mathias started to climb. The
rough stones were slippery but provided
enough footing. He reached the second floor
where a nearby eave wrapped around to the
front. He pulled himself up and sidestepped
across to where he could reach the over-
hanging roof. He grabbed onto the carved
wooden rafters and looked below. Devere
started to climb. Then Mathias hoisted himself up, swung a leg over the edge, and
pulled himself onto the snow-covered roof.
It was steeply pitched and he climbed carefully to the chimney. He crouched down
against the stone. Someone had a fire going
inside and the smoke smelled good in the
cold air.

Below him, Devere's glove appeared over
the edge of the roof. Then he pulled himself
into view and rolled onto the top. Mathias
signaled and Devere started to climb. He got
about halfway over when his left leg slipped
out beneath him. He flattened out against
the roof and started to slide down toward
the edge. He grabbed at the snow, but there
was nothing for him to hold on to. He

crossed over the edge, and the toe of his boot caught in the copper gutter. He came to a stop. The snow cascaded down. It landed softly on the terrace roof and apparently went unnoticed. He made his way up again and joined Mathias.

"I need a rag or scarf," Mathias said.

Devere looked puzzled, but he opened his jacket and patted down his pockets. He found a red nerkerchief. He handed it over.

Mathias unfolded the cloth on his knee, then he stood up and laid it out over the center flue of the chimney. The smoke started to curl around the edges, but he packed them down with snow and sealed it off.

"That's really going to improve the atmosphere inside," said Devere.

"I know." Mathias chuckled as the chimney began to back up. He leaned over the side of the roof and pointed to a narrow window that was about six feet down and said, "That's where we're going in. Brace yourself and lower me down."

Mathias's foot touched the wide windowsill. It was as far as Devere could lower him. He balanced himself while Devere dropped his legs over and then lowered himself down. He could just reach Mathias's shoulders with his feet, and used him as a middle step to the sill. Then, one on the left and one on the right, they steadied themselves.

Mathias leaned his head in slightly to see what was inside. The narrow window was at the end of a carpeted hallway. Halfway down, he could see a railing winding out around a staircase lit up from below.

Devere nudged Mathias. He nodded at the ground. One of the soldiers was passing beneath them. Both cadets pressed themselves as close to the window as possible. The guard turned the corner slowly and walked out of sight.

Mathias turned his attention back to the window when a piercing alarm rang through the lodge. The shrill sound split the silence and kicked off a total breakdown of order.

"Smoke alarm," Mathias said, smiling.

Without a second's hesitation, he kicked in the window and jumped through. Devere flew in behind him. They scrambled to their feet and raced down the hall to the head of the stairs.

Below, they saw soldiers and civilians alike running for the front door. Thick smoke filled the foyer. In the confusion, nobody noticed the cadets as they bounded down the steps across to the main reception room, where the smoke was the thickest.

Covering their mouths, they entered. In the middle of the room was a high-backed wooden chair facing away from them. They moved it around to find Crane, his arms and legs tied to the chair. His face was beaten and he was nearly unconscious.

"Crane! It's me, Mathias!" Mathias was shaking him. Devere was busy cutting him free.

Slowly, Crane opened his eyes. He tried to speak but couldn't. Then he coughed hard and gasped for breath.

"We got to get him out of here fast before he suffocates!" Mathias yelled. "Grab his arms."

They picked him up by his arms, wrapping one around each of their necks. Crane staggered to his feet, barely able to walk. Mathias noticed a door leading to the side veranda. They dragged him toward it.

Devere kicked the door open and they were outside. The cold fresh air nearly made them all dizzy after the thick smoke inside. Crane started coughing again.

Suddenly, they heard gunfire to their left.

"Move out! Move out!" Tyler yelled as he emerged from the tree line. He ran toward the large clearing in back of the lodge.

Mathias and Devere looked back and saw a large Soviet chopper approaching the hunting lodge fast. Soldiers were firing at it. The three took a firm hold of Crane and ran for the clearing.

Washuta had just circled over the roof and was setting down in the clearing as they came up. Tyler helped Mathias and Devere get Crane in the hatch, then hopped in themselves.

Tyler barely had time to get into the co-pilot's seat before Washuta took off. As he put on his headset, he looked down into the night and saw the Russian soldiers and civilians shooting up at them.

"Took you long enough, Washuta," Tyler said.

"Hey, Navy, without coordinates, even a hotdog like me has to scramble. How's our man Crane?"

Tyler turned around to see Devere giving him some mouth-to-mouth resuscitation, while Mathias was working his legs. It didn't look good.

"He's all beat up," Tyler clicked in. "We've got to get him some medical care, ASAP!"

"We'll be at the Otter in ten minutes."

Williams and Anderson had just finished loading the Soviet plane into the hold when they heard chopper rotors. Williams ran for his weapon while Anderson started up the engine. No way they were going to catch Soviet rockets for a bunch of green kid cadets.

The chopper appeared over the treetops, then circled the far bank, and headed in to set down on the ice, near the Otter. Washuta cut the engines, but left on the lights.

Mathias jumped out immediately in full view, with his arms up. Williams put down his weapon and motioned for them to hurry.

Tyler and Devere took Crane to the Otter. Mathias went back to grab the radio, then ran toward the seaplane.

"Where the hell's the pilot?" Williams yelled as the four cadets boarded.

Washuta had just jumped from the cockpit and was running toward the plane. He hopped aboard.

"Lock up and take off—fast!" he yelled at Williams.

Williams didn't respond.

"Look, man, I rigged the chopper to blow in five minutes, okay? Tell your pilot to take off, now!"

Williams nodded and ran toward the cockpit.

"How's Crane?" Washuta asked, fumbling with something in the pocket of his flight suit.

"He's not great, but it looks like he'll make it if we can get to the ship in time," Devere said.

Mathias turned toward Washuta. "How'd you rig the chopper to blow?"

"Easy," he said, pointing out the small window of the Otter. "Just before I jumped, I pushed the engines on full. Once the rotors start up, the wacked-out torques will tip her over and she'll go up. That way, the Ruskies'll think that we got killed in the crash. No loose ends.''

"Hey, Washuta, you just might have a future in this man's military," Tyler said, slapping him on the back.

Suddenly, they felt the plane move and took their seats. Anderson was taxiing off the bank and down the frozen river. As the cadets watched out the window, the trees along the bank became a green and white blur as the plane picked up speed.

But something was wrong. They weren't lifting off.

"Too much weight, with that damn plane in the hold," Washuta shouted over the engines. "He'll have to drop the extra fuel pods to get airborne."

Williams came running back through the aisles. He stopped at the stern of the hold and released two levers. The plane lurched, skidded, then steadied. Out the window, Washuta saw the two tanks bouncing on the ice as the plane picked up speed.

"All right! We'll be airborne any minute now." The other cadets held tight and waited for lift-off.

The Otter bounced twice before it finally took off and started to climb. Soon, they were above the trees, headed for the coast. The horizon was beginning to lighten into dawn.

Mathias looked back to see a red and orange glow against the dark sky. "There goes our loose ends, guys. A cool fifty million up in smoke."

ELEVEN

The sea was dark and rough as the Otter landed on its pontoons about a half a mile east of the U.S.S. *Orion*. Anderson signaled the ship for emergency pickup with medical assistance standing by.

Crane had come around a little during the flight. He still was breathing hard, but his eyes were open and he knew he was safe. The other cadets kept him awake by talking to him and shaking him if he looked like he was about to doze off.

After about twenty minutes, the *Orion* was alongside and the medical crew was taking Crane to sick bay. The cadets headed up the portside ladder. Almost immediately, a crane was lowered to extract the Otter's cargo.

The cadets were brought below to a briefing room. Hot coffee and eggs were waiting for them on a gray metal table off to one side.

"You men are to chow down, then wait here for Colonel Langstrom," the ensign said, then turned and left.

"Some heroes' welcome," Tyler said, joining the others as they took their food and sat around on chairs.

"That's nothing. There's still the colonel. He could have our butts for not following orders, losing valuable equipment, jeopardizing national security, endangering op personnel—"

"But we completed the mission, Mathias. We brought back nearly half the goddamn plane for him." Tyler stabbed at his mound of powdered eggs and soggy potatoes.

"You got that right," Devere agreed. "Langstrom's hardball, but he's got to cut us some slack on this."

"Dream on, dude," Washuta answered. "He could hang us out to dry."

Mathias stood. "Look, remember the plan. We never received the abort order because our radio was out. If we stick to that, we should be okay."

The rest of the cadets nodded halfheartedly and finished their breakfast in silence.

About half an hour later, the door banged open and the ensign stepped into the room. "Atten–hut!"

The cadets snapped into position, glancing at each other with anxious expressions.

"Here it comes," Tyler whispered to Washuta.

A second later, Colonel Charles Langstrom walked into the room. "That will be all, Ensign." The young man left, closing the door behind him.

Langstrom took his hat off and threw it on the table. It landed next to the coffeepot.

"Mathias, what were your orders?"

"Sir, to retrieve the flight box from a downed Soviet spy plane, to avoid all enemy contact, and to rendezvous at the designated pickup point in fourteen hours, sir." Mathias was trying to control the fear in his voice.

"What were your final orders, mister?"

Mathias looked puzzled. "Begging your pardon, sir. Final orders, sir?"

Langstrom let out a deep sigh. "Your final direct order was to abort the mission due to a change in object status. The order was transmitted in pulse code in response to your request for additional transport."

"Sir, I take responsibility for breaking radio silence. However, due to a malfunction in our radio equipment, no such final order was received. In view of the serious nature of our mission, I took command initiative to complete the operation according to a revised op plan.''

"I see,'' Langstrom answered skeptically. "I'll expect a full report from you on the specifics of this mission before we rendezvous with the U.S.S. *Concord* in four hours. Until we get to the carrier, you men are confined to quarters.''

"Sir, permission to ask a question.''

"Granted, Tyler.''

"Thank you, sir. What is the status of Cadet Crane, sir?''

"Crane suffered superficial face wounds and some smoke inhalation. He is expected to live.''

"All right!'' Washuta said, unable to control himself.

"What was that, Cadet?'' Langstrom said.

"Sorry, sir. Uh . . . the news about Crane . . . I guess I—''

"Understood,'' Langstrom cut him off. Washuta shut up fast.

The colonel walked over to retrieve his hat from the metal table, then moved toward the door. When he had his hand on the handle, he turned and stared at the cadets.

The boys were still at rigid attention. They tried to look straight ahead, but couldn't help glancing at each other and at Langstrom.

"My orders are to extend a discretionary

commendation upon the completion of this mission from the joint chiefs to the Talon Group.'' He saluted the boys, then added, directly at Mathias, "Damn shame the crew reported the field radio was lost overboard during the cargo transfer. Right, Mathias?"

"Yes, sir. Damn shame, sir." Mathias had a hard time controlling his grin as the colonel saluted and left.

The other cadets had no problem with theirs.

Join Colonel Langstrom and the Talon Group, five top U.S. cadets, on their next exciting mission to recover a South American dictator's cache of gold from his secret tropical island fortress:

**CADETS #2
CODE NAME: SAND CASTLE**

Boys' action, adventure, sports,
and mystery at their very best!

Five boys and their dirt bikes survive any way they
can in the tough, post-holocaust Mojave Desert.

A group of military cadets from elite U.S. academies
is ordered by the Pentagon on dangerous covert
missions to save the free world!

On the line and against the odds, the Tucker High
School football Tigers fight their way from the
underdog slot to the top of the league!

Chris and Ryan Taylor are as different as two thir-
teen-year-old fraternal twins can be. But each can
sense what the other is thinking and feeling, which
comes in handy when they're solving mysteries!